Model Number Unknown

Also by C.T. Carey

The Cantatio Tales

The Bard's Ballad

Children's Books

Jack B. Nymble Mysteries

The Mystery of the Missing Shoe

Model Number Unknown

C.T. Carey

ISBN: 978-1-7375722-8-2

*This book is dedicated to all the people
who have encouraged me through life*

*A special thank you to my parents who
have always helped me fulfill my dreams*

Tuesday Afternoon

Deputy Charles Harris Jr. sat there, innocently assuming that this shift would be just like any other shift. His partner, Deputy Pedro Gonzales, was in the passenger seat beside him, as usual. The two had spent many hours together in this radio car since being assigned as partners a little over two years ago.

In keeping with their daily routine they had stopped for coffee at the start of their shift, then stopped in a nearby parking lot, waiting for calls to come in, which didn't happen often.

Deputy Harris sipped on his usual drink: a scalding hot coffee with nothing in it. Just the way he liked it. Even as a teenager, when he first started to drink coffee, Harris never added anything to it. He truly just enjoyed the strong flavor of a good dark roast.

Deputy Gonzales, on the other hand, was enjoying an extra-large, triple shot, caramel swirl, blended mocha with whip cream. It was too much for one drink. At least that was Harris's opinion, which he jokingly shared on almost a daily basis.

Before they had sat for long, they found themselves handing out their first ticket of the day, a speeding ticket. Actually, it was their first ticket of the week.

Before long, there were only a few more hours until their shifts were over. They expected the day would end much like any other Tuesday. Not much happened on a Tuesday. Not much happened on any day if one were truly honest. When they had issued the speeding ticket, they had actually been quite surprised since, more often than not, the only type of calls they received were to help find a lost dog or give a talk at a middle school about career options.

"You got any plans tonight?" Gonzales asked Harris.

"Nah, nothing special," Harris replied. "I'll probably just stream a movie and order take-out. You know," he added with a cheerful laugh, "my usual. But how about you? How are things going with Lucy?" Lucy was Gonzales's long-time girlfriend.

"Lucy and I are great; we're going out tonight. She has been looking forward to it. I made reservations at *Chez l'amor* like a month ago. I guess I better remember which fork to use since she bought a new dress and even got me a tie to match. " Gonzales answered.

"Oooh, fancy. And matching outfits? Sounds serious, like taking Christmas card pictures together kinda serious," Harris said with a cheerful tone, happy for his partner to have possibly found the one. *Chez l'amor* was one of the nicest restaurants in town. It was very popular for dates and particularly for marriage proposals. "So I've heard that-"

Harris hadn't been able to finish his sentence. He was interrupted by a sharp, short, chirping sound that emitted from the dashboard speaker. Both deputies were startled a bit, confused for a moment as to where the sound came from. They then looked down at their console. Over two years, they had only heard that sound a few times.

As Harris looked down at the car's console, he heard a voice come over the radio. "Attention, all available units located near the vicinity of Maple Avenue and Birch Street. We have a report of a potential One-Eight-Seven, I repeat, One-Eight-Seven. All available units, please respond. Unit 7-Alpha, respond Code 3."

Harris and Gonzales glanced at each other, a look of confusion on their face. They were Unit 7-Alpha. This would be the first time they had ever been ordered to role code to a scene. And as it would turn out, this wasn't just any scene…

"One-Eight-Seven?" Gonzales asked. "What's that?"

"Check the manual," Harris replied as he put the car in drive. He had most of the codes memorized from his time at the academy, but he didn't recognize One-Eight-Seven. He was fairly confident he had never responded to such a call.

While Gonzales pulled out their manual, Harris pressed 'Acknowledged' on the console, then 'Navigate.' The built-in navigation appeared on the screen as he pulled the radio car out onto the street.

Harris flipped a switch on the console, instantly greeted by the wailing call of a siren while simultaneously, the swirl of blue and red lights flashed around them. He reached down to the radio, eyes still on the road, and raised the handset to his mouth. He calmy spoke into it. "This is Unit 7-Alpha. Deputies Harris and Gonzales. We are en route to the scene. ETA three minutes."

"One-Eight-Five… One-Eight-Six…" Gonzales muttered to himself as he flipped through a small book. "One-Eight-Seven, here we go." Harris could hear Gonzales mumble something.

"What was that?" Harris asked.

Gonzales was silent for a moment, looked over to Harris, and said very solemnly. "One-Eight-Seven. Homicide." Harris looked to Gonzales's eyes wide with concern.

"Homicide?" Harris questioned as he looked back to the road. "I thought there weren't supposed to be things like that here."

"I thought so too…" Gonzales replied, clearly a million things running through his mind.

The citizens of Politopia had been told they wouldn't experience crime. The official crest of Politopia bore the phrase '*I Gi Chorís Psegádi*' after all. It was Greek for '*The Land Without Blemish.*'

A homicide seemed like a pretty significant blemish, Harris thought to himself.

Several other deputies reported that they would arrive at the crime scene shortly. Harris and Gonzales looked at each other once more and rode the rest of the way to the scene in silence. Neither of them knew what to think, and neither of them knew what to expect.

Homicide Detective Lewis Halistad had been listening to the scanner when the call was sent out about the homicide.

Less than a minute later, he received a call over his private frequency.

"Detective Halistad," the voice said. "We have a highly probable homicide at Maple Avenue and Birch Street. We need you to respond. CSI will be at the scene as well to assist you."

Halistad pursed his lip and slowly nodded his head, "Copy, responding now." He put the handset down and muttered to himself, "I didn't think I would have to deal with this."

He was actually in the vicinity of the scene and was there in mere minutes, pulling his car up to a residential home. It was one story and couldn't be more than two bedrooms. From the solitude of his car, he observed the scene. There was a lot of movement taking place. The front door was wide open, with a constant stream of deputies coming and going. There were about half a dozen deputies and a few CSI agents. The responding deputies that had arrived at the scene first had already set up a perimeter. Several of them now were having to push the media back behind the crime scene tape. Halistad walked to the scene, trying to look as unimportant as possible. He knew the media would be all over him as soon as they saw him. Despite his efforts to blend into the swarm of deputies, one of the local media representatives recognized him, shouting out to him as she hurried towards him.

"Detective Halistad. Detective!" she called again when he didn't stop. The reporter ran, catching up to Halistad, then matched his pace. "Does the agency have anything they can report at this time?" She had a note pad and pen ready, expecting to get something she could use for the evening news.

"I'm sorry," Halistad said without looking at her. "You'll have to speak to the agency public information officer." When he came to the tape, he flashed his badge to a deputy standing in the yard. The deputy took a note on his clipboard and waved Halistad past.

The detective continued to the house without breaking stride and heard the deputy say to the reporter, "I'm sorry, ma'am, but this is an active crime scene. You'll have to remain with the rest of the reporters and wait for the department public information officer to make an official statement."

"Anything? Has a weapon been discovered?" She begged to the deputy, "Can we at least have a name?"

Halistad continued on his path and could faintly hear the deputy dismissing the woman again just as the detective went through the front door into the threshold of death.

Deputy Harris had just managed to get rid of the reporter. He handed his clipboard off to another deputy and hurried to catch up with Detective Halistad. Halistad was already in the foyer of the home when Harris came up behind him.

"Detective Halistad," he said to get the detective's attention. "Deputy Harris," he continued, introducing himself.

"My partner Gonzales and I were the first to arrive at the scene. It seems that a neighbor reported seeing, what she called, a 'shady figure' leaving the building about an hour ago. She called the victim's house phone several times, but he never picked up. She came over to knock on the door but was surprised when she found it ajar. She knocked and called out, but still no response. She opened the door and called in again. She was planning on locking up in case the victim had left the door open when he left," Harris was reading from a notepad. "She said she had a key for when the victim was on vacation. She was about to close the door and lock it when she saw something on the kitchen floor. She went in to look and quickly realized that it was a body. She panicked and ran home, leaving the door open. She called it in immediately."

Halistad nodded his head and headed to the kitchen, which was through an open doorway directly to the right of the foyer. Harris followed after the detective and continued, "My partner Gonzales is interviewing the neighbor now and will get her to sign an official statement."

"Anything else?" Halistad asked. They were now standing in the kitchen. The body was still lying on the floor. Harris had to swallow down bile the first time he had entered the kitchen. It was the first dead body he'd ever seen, other than photographs and television. And this was a particularly gruesome one to see. There was a bloody gash on the neck and a pool of now congealing blood. Even now, Harris couldn't bring himself to look at it.

"Victim appears to be James McGrundy," Harris continued. "His friends called him Jimmy, age 28. Model number is yet to be identified. However, the neighbor gave a visual identification, and we found a wallet with an ID on the entry table."

"Have you found a weapon?" Halistad was now walking circles around the body, staying well away from the puddle of blood.

"Yes, sir," responded Deputy Harris. "When we came in, Gonzales noticed that a knife was missing from the block," Harris pointed to the counter where the knife block was, "We checked the sink, assuming it had been used, but it wasn't there either. We found the knife halfway under the couch in the living room." Halistad went that way, and a crime scene investigator came into the kitchen and began photographing and marking evidence.

Halistad went to the knife and picked it up to examine it. There were still remnants of blood on the blade, and Halistad could see matching stains on the carpet where it had been dropped. Halistad was rotating the knife, looking at it from all angles.

Harris coughed and said nervously, "Detective." He cast his eyes down. "Shouldn't you be wearing gloves? Fingerprints haven't been taken yet."

Halistad cursed and dropped the knife back to the ground. Gruffly he asked, "When's the coroner going to arrive?"

"They said he should be here soon." Harris followed Halistad back to the kitchen as the crime scene investigator went to the living room and began photographing the knife. Harris fell back and whispered to the investigator, making sure Halistad couldn't hear, and told him of the knife mix-up. The investigator wrote it in a notebook, and Harris caught up to Halistad.

Halistad was back at the corpse, examining the body closely, peering at the face. "So we don't have a model number yet?"

"No, sir," Harris answered. "I managed to get in contact with a National Creation Department representative, but because of the Creation Protection Act, they can't disclose model numbers without a whole load of paperwork. They're a pain in the you-know-what. I'm already on it, though. We should have an answer within a few days, hopefully sooner. I went to school with someone who works there, and they might be able to pull a few strings."

"Fine. I want that report as soon as it becomes available, and I'll want the official statement of the neighbor as well. Get them to me the second they become available." Halistad stood up and looked at Harris, "You ever worked a homicide case before, Harris?"

"No… No sir, first I've heard of one happening," Harris replied, confused.

"Oh, right. You're part of the 'Perfect Population.'" Halistad said to himself, then he looked back to Harris, "I've seen dozens like this outside. You've handled it well."

"Thank you, sir. Let me know any way I can assist," Harris responded.

"Like I said, all those reports as soon as they become available." With that, Halistad left the crime scene and went back to his non-descript blue sedan.

The same reporter from before noticed him and hurried over to him. Detective Halistad managed to close the door of the car just before the reporter got to him. He started the car and drove away.

"I can't believe they called me in for this one. 'Utopia,'" he laughed. "I don't think anyone will call this place a utopia anymore."

He drove past the command post, then sped down the road, heading towards home. He knew there would be a lot of work to do.

Harris was still at the scene two hours later. The coroner had arrived at this point and was able to place the time of death between 1715 and 1845, which corroborated the neighbor's testimony. The neighbor had put the time of death around 1805. The neighbor was very sure of the time as her soap opera had just come on. The coroner was also able to confirm that the neck wound was the cause of death.

"Massive bleeding," he said. "It was an extremely deep wound. It hit the carotid. Likely went unconscious in a minute and bled to death just a few moments after."

The crime scene had been thoroughly swept. The only thing particularly out of the ordinary was the bloody knife. A crime scene investigator had thoroughly photographed the blade and then bagged and tagged it. Harris saw him put a bright orange sticker on it that read, 'Contaminated,' and the investigator wrote 'Halistad' on the label.

Harris left the crime scene and found Gonzales still outside in the yard. The media had finally left the scene. He could already imagine the headlines for tomorrow, "Murder in Paradise" or "Utopian Homicide."

"Gonzales!" Harris called to his partner, "I've got a ton of paperwork to file, and you've got your date. Let's roll." Gonzales jogged over to Harris. The deputies went back to their radio car to roll back to the station. Harris reached down to take a sip of his coffee and was disappointed to find it cold now. He looked over and saw that Gonzales's mocha had melted whip, and all the caramel had sunk to the bottom of the clear plastic cup.

"It's hard to believe that just a few hours ago, we had nice drinks, and neither of us had ever seen a real dead body," Gonzales said quietly. "Nothing has really changed, but somehow everything feels… different." He shrugged, clearly at a loss for how to explain his feelings.

Harris nodded his head slowly in agreement while lost in his own thoughts.

"You think it will change anything with Politopia?" Gonzales's voice was sad and soft. "I mean, doesn't this make the whole thing a failure?"

Harris thought about the question. Dr. Kolifax had created Politopia to be a place without illness, without crime, and without violence. He hypothesized that if he made the perfect person, no one would turn to crime.

Until today there really wasn't any need for the police force at all if one were truly honest. The most that Harris had ever dealt with were a couple of minor disputes and some petty shoplifting. Never anything violent. There were less than a few dozen deputies on the police force in total. There just isn't a need for any more than that. "*Wasn't* a need," Harris said aloud.

"What was that?" Gonzales asked, looking up from his drink.

"Oh, sorry. I was just thinking out loud." He was brought back to reality and told Gonzales, "I don't know if it will actually change anything. I doubt it. One murder doesn't ruin all of Politopia." Gonzales could tell Harris didn't truly mean it, but both of them were too conflicted to admit anything aloud.

Upon arriving back at the station, they changed out of their uniforms, and gave them to the complimentary dry-cleaning service, then went their separate ways.

Fortunately, they had managed to leave soon enough that Gonzales was still able to make it to his date with his girlfriend at *Chez l'amor*.

Harris began driving home but then decided that he would stream a movie another night. Right now, he didn't want to be alone with his thoughts or the images in his head. He decided that he really wanted to see his parents.

Well, they weren't exactly his parents, at least not in the biological sense of the word. Harris was part of the new "Created" population. Dr. Kolifax had been madly working on cloning for years. He managed to take the idea of cloning from the world of science-fiction and literature it had always been regarded as and bring the concept to life by introducing it into the world of genetics. Kolifax had a fascination to the point of obsession with eugenics. This called for arranged mating in order to form the most ideal human. While Dr. Kolifax favored the idea of an ideal human, he didn't want forced reproduction. Instead, he desired to make the perfect specimen himself. Through his research, Kolifax found a single strand of DNA present in every living human. He called it the 'Foundation DNA,' or F-DNA, as most now referred to it. With this discovery, he was able to take the F-DNA and make it into a serum which was the basis of all created humans. This allowed Kolifax to clone someone rapidly and even modify their DNA to perfection. He took out all mutations and illnesses and made the ideal person.

After making this breakthrough, he found prime specimens from the "real" population, using them as the basis of his new utopia. Dr. Kolifax recruited warriors, artists, performers, scientists, mathematicians. All the best, brightest, and accomplished in their field. He insisted on perfection in physical appearance as well. Beauty, muscle mass, bone structure, teeth, and hair. It was all, well, perfect. After manipulating their genetic make-up, Kolifax was finally able to create models of these specimens. Designing what he thought was "The Perfect Population." In the early stages, each of his clones was named "P.S.," which was an abbreviation for Perfect Specimen. The doctor created a program so incredibly complex and yet so easy to implement. All he or his team had to do was take a predetermined solution, mix it with the F-DNA extraction, put the mixed concoction into a special incubator, and then, voila! They had an infant P.S.

Despite being made in a lab, the Perfect Specimens were still fully human. There were just… well… They were perfect. Free of diseases, mentally and physically sharp. Kolifax then created model numbers, each based on a 'real' person and each one with a specific set of abilities. Some were designed to be athletes; others were artists or doctors. Whatever their predetermined role in society was, every one of the models was assigned a three-digit code. The codes were then used to identify them for their intended purpose.

For example, Model 313 was intended for educators. Model 282 created writers and poets. Model 153 were computer scientists and programmers. Model 101 made animal trainers and equestrian experts. There were hundreds of models. They were consistently rotated through and updated. Every possible need was thought of. The most recent model was Model 796, which created fashion designers.

With the advent of Perfect Specimens, Politopia was born. Naturally, Dr. Kolifax didn't want his perfect humans living amongst and breeding naturally or even being destroyed by just immediately joining the world's population of "regular" people.

Now, there were some "regular" people living in Politopia, of course, some of the humans he used the DNA of, and some chosen few to help raise the population of Perfect Specimens. However, Dr. Kolifax still hoped that the entire population would be perfect one day. While it wasn't outlawed, traditional reproduction was now faux pas; instead, adopting a P.S. was the way of life in Politopia. Who wouldn't want a perfect child, after all?

Harris's parents were part of the small group of regular people living in Politopia. They had come to the utopia during the first round of creation. Before any knowledge of Politopia existed, it had been discovered that they were unable to conceive a child together. They had been on waiting lists for years in hopes of adopting a child to complete their dreams of what they thought of as a perfect family. Eventually, they heard of and met Dr. Kolifax. The doctor told them about Politopia, insisting that they would be able to start their dream family as soon as they were citizens of this new, perfect city. Upon hearing they would be able to adopt a child there, nothing else mattered. They immediately left their "regular" lives behind, heading for this utopia.

Soon after, as promised, they were able to adopt an infant, a Perfect Specimen. They named him Charles Harris Jr., after his new adoptive father. While they weren't his natural parents, they loved him more than anything. Truly as if he were their own. Better still, Harris loved them in just the same way, never thinking of them as anything other than his mom and dad.

Harris was part of the first batch of created humans. He was created as a Model 353. This particular model was designed to create powerful and fearless men. Model 353 developed P.S. into everything from top physical athletes to police officers.

P.S. could still do as they wished, though.

Being created as a specific model number didn't always seal the deal on their future. The P.S. humans, while perfect, still had free will. Politopia was intended to be a utopia, after all.

Dr. Kolifax felt that not allowing for free will was taking away one of human's greatest abilities. The ability to choose. He firmly believed that by being perfect and growing up in a perfect nurturing environment, one would develop into their predetermined and cultivated role in society.

Harris knew other P.S. that had chosen lives other than their model numbers intention. His partner, Deputy Gonzales, was a Model 227.

It was well known that Model 227 had been designed for entertainers and performers. But as Gonzales grew up, he found he had more desire to be a deputy than to dance on stage.

Tuesday Night

Harris drove down the quiet, peaceful, residential street that led to his parents' house. He pulled his car into the driveway, just as he always did. They always left him a space in the driveway, telling him he was welcome to come home anytime.

It was getting later in the evening, and Harris wasn't sure if his parents were asleep, so he used his key to unlock the door. He was surprised to find that they were still awake and in the living room.

They were watching one of their family's favorite shows about an older woman who seemed to always be finding dead bodies and then solving the subsequent homicide case. After today, Harris couldn't imagine seeing more than one dead body in a lifetime.

"Honey!" Harris's mom called when she saw him. She got up and ran to give him a hug. "What are you doing here? Did we miss a call?" She started to pull out her phone, intending to see when she had missed a call from Harris. Before she could, Harris stopped her.

"No. This was very last minute. I just needed a comforting place to be. I had a bit of a hectic day today. I need to make some phone calls and then file a bunch of paperwork."

His dad paused the show and turned to Harris, "Well, what's going on, son?"

"I don't know if I'm really allowed to talk about it…"

Harris's mom, Petunia, guided him over to the couch and motioned for Harris to sit down next to her. "At least tell us what you can."

"Okay, this all has to be confidential." They nodded in agreement, so Harris continued. "There was a murder."

His mom gasped, "Who was it? A politician, a dignitary, some celebrity?" Those inside Politopia still got news of the outside world, but for the most part, they were disconnected and only heard of the big scandals.

"No, Mom, it was here… in Politopia."

Even his dad's breath caught this time. "You don't say. How?"

"Stabbing. I just left the scene. It's not official yet, but the victim was James McGrundy."

Petunia gasped again, "Oh, poor Jimmy." In response to Harris's confused look, she continued, "His mother, Jamie McGrundy, and I play bridge together. She and Bill, Jimmy's dad, are…uh…regular people like us." She reached over and grabbed Charles Sr.'s hand.

"Any suspects, son?" Charles Sr., or Chuck as most people called him, asked.

"None. A neighbor reported seeing a shady figure leaving the house. She went over to check on Jimmy and found his body."

"That must have been Gertrude," Petunia said. "She and Jimmy's mom grew up together in the real world. Gertrude moved here with them, and she always looked after Jimmy. She was like an aunt to him."

Harris suddenly had an idea. "Are you very close to Jamie?"

His mom shrugged and replied, "Well, we are friends. I'm not sure how close that is."

He asked, "Any chance you know what Jimmy's model number is?"

"Sorry, honey, I don't. We regular people don't really think about model numbers and serums and all that. Jamie and Bill were like us, as far as I know, always wanting a child and finally getting one. All they cared about was having Jimmy." Harris saw a tear forming in the corner of his mother's eye.

"That's alright, Mom. Thanks anyway. In that case, I have a few phone calls I need to make. Is my room still set up?"

"Of course it is," Petunia said, "In fact, I just washed the bedding yesterday if you'd like to stay the night. And I have some clothes for you in the dresser."

"Thanks, Mom. I think I'll take you up on that offer." Harris headed back to his room and pulled out his phone.

He made several calls, but each of them was without a positive result. Finally, Harris decided to call his friend at the National Creation Department.

The NCD dealt with all paperwork and reports pertaining to Kolifax's work, including the creation of the Perfect Specimens.

The phone rang a few times when Harris heard it pick up, "Is that you, Charles?" Harris hadn't been called Charles by anyone but his parents in quite a while. Everyone on the force called him by his last name. "It's been a while."

Harris could hear a video game playing in the background. David had always been a fan of video games all through high school.

"Hey, David." Harris said, "I need a favor, off-the-record. It's important."

"Can it wait a few minutes? I'm about to beat this level. I've been working on it for weeks," David said, sounding distracted.

"It's serious, and it all has to stay off the record until official papers are filed."

Harris heard the video game stop, and David said, "You sound serious. What's up?"

"It has to do with the NCD."

"Oh, work talk, fun," David remarked sarcastically.

"I know. As I said, this has to be totally off the record. There's been a homicide. Here, in Politopia. We can't get an answer on what the victim's model number is. I tried making a few phone calls, but everything has come up dead ends from the Creation Protection Act."

The CPA had been put in place to protect P.S.'s rights to privacy as to what model they were.

David sighed, "Oh yeah, pretty hard to get around that. You have a name?"

"Yeah, James McGrundy, male, 28 years old. Is there any way you can get that number without all the paperwork and waiting?"

"Well, I don't have access to that information myself. But what I can do is expedite things significantly. I'll still need all the paperwork, though. If you can get the paperwork to me by morning, I might be able to have a number for you as soon as tomorrow evening."

"You're a miracle worker David. Thanks, and say hi to Millie and the kids for me."

"Will do, Harris," David said. "Make sure to tell your mom and dad I say hello as well."

Harris heard the sound of video games begin once more and hung up the phone.

Harris realized it had been quite a while since he had seen David. "Was it really his wedding?" Harris said out loud. Harris had been the best man at David's wedding and now wasn't sure if he'd seen him since. David and Harris had been best friends all through high school. They had been on football and baseball teams together, had crushes on the same girls, and overall had been as close as brothers. David was a model number 210, which often led to bureaucrats. Being close friends with Harris, though, David had tried out for the police force but didn't make it through training.

He then joined the National Creation Department, worked his way up the ranks, married his high school sweetheart, and had a few kids. His wife, Millie, and he had one kid the traditional way, then chose to adopt two P.S. children.

They had texted a few times since David's weddings, but only on their birthdays. David and his wife always sent out Christmas cards, but that was the only communication they'd had for years.

Harris forced himself to stop reminiscing and pulled his laptop out of his bag. He logged onto the NCD website and found the forms he needed. He would print three total: one requesting model number, another for a CPA by-pass, and a final for a non-familial relations request.

Harris still heard the T.V. playing in the living room and went out to see his parents. Walking into the living room, he found his dad snoring on the couch while his mom was still awake, knitting a blanket.

"Hey, Mom," Harris whispered, not wanting to wake his dad. "Is the printer still set up in the office? I need to print some forms."

"It is, sweetie. We just got a new one. Apparently, it prints twice as fast, but I don't see a difference."

Harris smiled and took his laptop to the office. He wirelessly connected it to the printer and hit print. While the forms were printing, Harris filed his official report of the crime scene.

A quarter of an hour, and 76 pages, later, Harris began filling out the forms. Harris was able to log into a secure platform on his laptop to view the crime scene photos, one of which was Jimmy's driver's license, which gave Harris his creation date and license number.

Harris finally finished the request and CPA by-pass forms and was just moving on to the non-familial request when he heard a knock on the office door. His mom cracked the door open, holding two glass bowls in her hands.

"I thought you might like some dessert," she said kindly.

Harris looked at the time. 0038. Just after midnight. He hadn't realized how long he'd been dealing with this paperwork. He looked to the stack left to complete. There were only a half dozen pages left, and most looked fairly simple. He decided he had time for a break.

"I'd love some. Thanks, Mom. What'd you make?"

"Cornbread with braised peaches, molasses, and homemade whip cream." It was a dessert they had a lot when Harris was a kid. Petunia made the best chili he'd ever had and often made a whole pan of delicious cornbread to go with it. She often found other uses for all the left-over cornbread. Harris's favorite was when his mom would make a sort of rustic strawberry shortcake with cornbread. It was surprisingly delicious and worthy of being added to Petunia's recipe book. The recipe book was special to their family because Petunia had received it from her mom when she and Chuck moved to Politopia.

"Delicious. Does this cornbread mean you made your chili today?" Harris asked hopefully. He realized he'd never had dinner and couldn't think of anything that sounded better than his mom's cooking.

"I thought you might ask that, one moment." Petunia disappeared and then came back with another bowl of chili topped with sour cream, cheese, and a healthy helping of green onions.

Harris set his cornbread dessert aside and devoured the bowl of chili. He then switched back to the cornbread and found the whipped cream slightly melted. The whole time Petunia had been slowly eating her own bowl of peach cornbread.

Harris and his mother didn't say anything while eating. They just sat together. They did that often. It was safe and comforting to just… be.

When Harris finished his cornbread, he stacked his bowls together and asked, "Do you want help with the dishes, Mom?"

"That's fine, honey, I'll take care of them," she took his bowls and stacked her's with them.

"I should probably send your father off to bed, and I know you have a lot of work to do," she left the room and asked, "You want me to close the door?"

"Yes, please. Thanks, Mom," and with that, Harris returned to his work. Fortunately, he only had those few last pages, and it turned out they were, in fact, pretty simple. First, he had to explain the reason for his request. Then, he had to fill out a separate page with his badge ID number and personal contact information.

With that, he scanned them all back to the computer and emailed them off to David. Lastly, he sent a text to David that said: *Documents sent. Thanks for the help.*

Less than a minute later, he got back: *No problem. We'll have to catch up soon, non-work-related. Now get some sleep.*

Harris looked at the clock again and saw that it was almost 0230. He texted back: *Agreed. After all this is done.*

Harris shut his laptop down and plugged in his phone. He took a quick, scalding hot shower to wash the day away, then slipped into his warm bed.

Detective Halistad had been waiting to view the crime scene evidence. He had set his email to alert him whenever something was added to the secure network. He heard a ding come from his phone and quickly logged into the site. He scrolled through the database down to 'McGrundy, James' and double-clicked it. Unfortunately, there wasn't much available yet.

The coroner had verified the cause of death as massive bleeding from a neck wound. The crime scene photos had been uploaded as well. Halistad scrolled through them: front door, the bloodied knife, dozens of pictures of the body, and other trivial photos. One thing Halistad particularly noted was that the fingerprints had come back. The detective read the report.

"Due to contamination at the crime scene, no definitive fingerprints have been determined from the knife," Halistad began to read the rest out loud to himself. "Detective Halistad's prints were found on the weapon from contamination, as mentioned above. Slight smearing of Halistad's prints is visible.

"The only other prints at the scene are those of neighbor Gertrude Heelson, which are present on the front door handle. As no other prints have been found at the crime scene, it is likely that the suspect wore gloves and/or wiped knife and other surfaces of prints." Halistad then quietly read through the neighbor's statement but didn't glean anything new from it other than she saw a tall, heavy-set figure leaving the house, but she couldn't tell anything else about them.

Finally, Halistad read through the official report and saw that it was submitted by Deputy Charles Harris Jr. He shook his head and, with a grim smirk, walked away.

"Seems like a cold case in the making to me," he said to himself.

Wednesday Morning

Harris slept through the night, but his dreams were filled with visions of Jimmy's dead body lying in the kitchen. Harris had joined the police force wanting to make a positive change and ensure that Politopia remained what it was: a perfect and flawless land. But he never thought something as filthy as murder could happen here.

Harris finally awoke to the sound of chirping birds as the first rays of sun broke through the window. He laid awake in bed for several minutes, alone with his thoughts, when he finally forced himself out of bed. Harris didn't have anywhere, in particular, to be until the evening. That's when his next shift started. He was relieved he could spend some time with his parents until then.

He opened his bedroom door, and could hear the TV on in the living room, and was welcomed by the smell of his mom's homemade buttermilk waffles. He walked down the hall, wearing basketball shorts and a tank top his mom had put in the dresser for him. It was the middle of summer, and even with the air conditioner running, it was still hot in the house. Harris thought he might even have time to go outback and work on the tan he was trying to gain. While Harris was quite muscular from his daily workouts and demanding job, he was well aware his skin was looking quite pale after the long winter months.

Harris came to the kitchen and found his mom cooking breakfast. "Need any help?" he offered while pouring himself a large mug of coffee, grateful his mom had already brewed a pot.

"I'm fine, honey. Everything should be done soon," his mom replied. "Your father is in the living room watching TV if you'd like to join him."

He nodded his head, sipping his coffee, heading to join his father.

In the living room, Harris was greeted by a photo of Jimmy McGrundy's body on the television. He watched for a moment, and then Chuck noticed that Harris had come into the room. Harris's dad reached for the remote to change the channel. "You probably don't want to hear any more about that," he said apologetically.

"No, it's fine, Dad. Leave it on. I want to hear what they're saying." Harris walked over to sit on the couch beside his father.

"Yesterday, a tragedy occurred," the newscaster said on the screen. It was the same reporter that had confronted Harris and chased after Halistad the day before. Harris read the banner at the bottom of the screen. 'Homicide in Politopia.' Harris was somewhat disappointed that they hadn't come up with a better tagline.

"A 28-year-old man was murdered in his own home. The family has been notified but does not wish to appear on television.

They just hope that nothing like this happens again. We have attempted to get an official statement from the police department. So far, we have been told that the victim is James McGrundy. The death came from a severe knife wound to the neck. It is unknown if the murder was premeditated or not. There are no official suspects yet, but we assure you we will keep the public notified of any new information." They switched to a human-interest story about some dog that could bark Mozart. Harris laughed, and Chuck turned the television off.

At about the same time, Petunia entered the living room to let Harris and Chuck know that breakfast was ready. They happily followed her to the dining room. Harris was greeted by a table full of waffles, bacon, eggs, several syrups, and more of the braised peaches from the previous night.

Harris was grateful for such a complete meal. Once he had moved out and was living on his own, he felt he mostly survived off of take-out and delivery. He was a decent cook. Who wouldn't be after watching his mother cook for so many years? He just never found that he had the time, or made the time, to cook a full meal just for him to eat alone.

Harris loaded his plate with several waffles and topped them with a helping of peaches and a drizzle of vanilla-infused maple syrup. Beside that, he placed a mound of eggs and several slices of bacon. He drizzled more maple syrup over these as well. A lot of people thought maple syrup on eggs was strange, but Harris would always tell them to try it before they judged.

They all ate until Petunia eventually broke the silence. She asked Harris, "Do you have any plans today, honey? Are you working on the case?"

Harris shook his head slowly and swallowed the food in his mouth. "I don't know. I haven't heard anything from anyone. I'm waiting to get a model number for James. I managed to get ahold of an old friend, and he's going to expedite things for me, but other than that, there aren't any leads at all. I suppose Detective Halistad, who's in charge of the case, will want to interview other neighbors, but other than that, I can't be sure. We've never gone through this before."

"Well, please, honey, let us know what we can do for you," his mom said. "And feel free to stay here as long as you'd like." His dad nodded his head in agreement.

He thought for a moment. The idea of staying here longer sounded really enjoyable. It meant he would have a little bit longer of a drive to the station, but it was worth being with family. "I'd like that. Thanks, Mom. If you don't mind, could I set up a sort of personal headquarters in the office? Maybe I can try to figure some other things out."

"Of course, it's not like either of us use it," she said with a laugh, putting her hand on Chuck's forearm.

They all finished their meal, and his mom washed all the dishes, despite Harris's insistence he wanted to do so. While his mom washed the dishes, Harris and his dad took some time to play video games together. It was something they enjoyed doing when Harris was younger, and it was nice to have it be like old times. Today they decided on a racing game they both loved. People were often surprised to discover that Harris's "old man" could play video games well, but he actually beat Harris quite often. And today was one of those days.

"Have you been practicing?" Harris asked accusatorily with a laugh. He was several laps behind Chuck and couldn't seem to catch up. It seemed that Chuck knew where every shortcut was and knew exactly which turns to take sharp and which ones to take wide.

"Maybe," Chuck replied with a mischievous grin.

They played for quite a while, enjoyed time by the pool, they even had lunch together poolside until Harris had to start getting ready for his shift. He would change at work, but he still loaded his bag up with his phone and laptop, along with the physical copies of the forms he'd sent David. He planned to add them to the official folder when he got to the station.

Wednesday Afternoon

Harris was driving to the station when his phone started to ring. He looked at the caller ID and saw that it was David calling. So he answered and clicked it onto speaker.

"Hey, David. Got anything for me?"

"You alone?" David asked, sounding nervous.

"Yeah, I'm in my car. Why? Did something happen?"

"I have to make it super clear this stays just between us. No one can know about this… before I tell you anything, you have to agree."

Harris was intrigued by what could be so secretive, "Yeah, sure. Do you want me to pinky-promise?"

David didn't laugh and continued seriously, "Alright, it seems that Jimmy McGrundy was a Model 353."

"Ok. But… why is this so hush-hush? Isn't this all info in the report we will get?"

"Well, I wasn't able to get an official report quickly. It's still going to take some processing time," David said. "But I may have accidentally looked over my boss's shoulder, and I just happened to memorize his password, and the next thing I knew, I was in the extreme lockdown files."

Harris hadn't realized David would have to do something like that and risk his job for him. It made him feel all the more guilty for not reaching out more often.

"Are you sure you won't get in trouble for that?" Harris really appreciated David's help, but he imagined all David would do was mark the request as 'Urgent.' He didn't imagine David would take it to such an extreme level. David really was a great friend.

"Nah, I should be fine. I made sure to encode my IP address before logging in. But, like I said, you didn't hear this from me, but I wanted to get the info to you as soon as possible."

"I'm just here. Sitting in my car. Talking to myself." Harris said.

"Eh. What's new?" David said with a laugh. It was the first time David had broken away from seriousness on the call. "So this will stay between you and me, right? You won't even tell the Sheriff that you have the number? The official report will be ready in a few days, and then, of course, everyone will know."

Harris's moral compass was spinning as if near a magnet. On the one hand, wasn't it his responsibility to share what he knew? On the other, he didn't want to destroy his friends' life getting him fired and possibly sent to jail.

"Yeah, of course, David," he said. He decided to go with friendship. It was just the model number. It didn't have that much significance in the case, and besides, detectives had confidential informants all the time. "I really owe you, David. Big time. I appreciate it."

"No worries. It was actually kind of fun, like a super high-stakes video game. Who knew those skills could be useful? Let me know if you need anything else."

"Will do," Harris said and then heard David end the call. He used a voice-activated assistant and heard his phone start to ring.

His mom picked up after only two rings, "Is everything okay, honey."

"Yeah, Mom, I'm fine. I just had a question. By any chance, do you know what Jimmy did? Like, did he have a career?"

"I'm pretty sure he was an athlete of some sort. I want to say hockey. I don't think he had played for at least a few years, though. He had some kind of injury several years ago and has been living off of medical retirement since then. Why do you ask? Something with the case?"

"Maybe, I don't know yet." Harris said, "While we're talking. Could you think, and maybe ask Jamie too, if anyone might have had a grudge against him? Maybe an old teammate? Or a rival player from another team?" He added quickly, "I hope that's not too much to ask."

"No trouble at all, dear. Jamie and I were going to play bridge this afternoon anyways. Stay safe at work, dear. I love you."

"I love you too, Mom." Harris ended the call and then pulled into the station parking lot. Hurrying in, he changed into his uniform and then gave the forms to a secretary to scan in and file.

She gave the originals back to Harris. He met Gonzales at their radio car. Harris took the keys and started the engine up, pulling onto the street. It seemed Gonzales was still affected from the day before, and they rode in silence.

They drove through a coffee stand, as was their routine. Harris ordered his usual, a black drip coffee, and Gonzales ordered his usual as well, a triple shot caramel swirl mocha, blended.

They drove away, and Harris took a large drink of his coffee. Gonzales half-heartedly took a sip of his drink.

"You good?" Harris asked Gonzales.

"I think so. I've just been thinking, I mean, am I really cut out for this? I'm a 227, after all. I'm supposed to dance and sing on stage or act on a screen. I'm not supposed to be a cop. It's not what I'm meant for."

Harris pulled the car to the side of the road and turned in his seat to look at Gonzales. "Don't let a number tell you what you can be. Take Fiona, for example. One of the greatest singers of our time, you know what her model number is?" Gonzales shrugged, "She's a number 478, for pete's sake. She should be in a laboratory discovering a new element or creating an even smaller cell phone. She didn't let a number tell her what she was going to be. And you shouldn't either. You got me?"

Gonzales nodded his head, "Yeah, I guess you're right. Fiona is pretty amazing... and hot."

Harris started the car and pulled back onto the road, "Don't you have a girlfriend?"

"That doesn't mean I'm blind. And anyways, even Lucy would admit Fiona is hot."

Harris and Gonzales laughed and continued their route. It was a very anticlimactic day comparatively to the previous one. There were no significant incidences for them today. They had a couple of speeding tickets and one missing person's report. But it ended up only being a mom who thought her son was missing, but he was actually just hiding in the laundry room closet on the top shelf.

Gonzales and Harris finished their shift without any more drama and drove back to the station. They changed and walked to the parking lot together.

"Where you off to?" Gonzales asked.

"My parents, I decided to stay with them for a few days. You?"

"Another date with Lucy. We're seeing *Friends Between Time*, some chick flick. I'd rather see *Galaxy Battle XII* but this week was her pick." Gonzales shrugged and climbed into his car.

Harris was about to get into his when he heard his name called.

"Harris!" Halistad called to Deputy Harris. "Do you have that report for me yet? Any identification on a model number yet?"

Harris turned to look back, "No sir, no report available yet. I'll let you know as soon as one comes in, though."

"That friend of yours able to help out?"

"He said he'd do whatever he could. I can call him again if you'd like," Harris replied.

"Do that. And if anything else comes in pu-"

Harris interrupted, "On your desk. Yes sir. Will do."

Harris climbed into his car and drove away.

"Dang bureaucrats. It takes forever to get a simple three-digit code." Halistad said as he returned to his office, ready to comb over the statement he had gotten from James's other neighbors. He was hoping there may be something in them that would point to the killer, but if he was being honest, he doubted it.

Harris had been running the conversation through his head the entire way back to his parents' house. Was it the right thing to have lied to Halistad?

Well, to be honest, he hadn't really lied. Halistad had asked for the report, which didn't exist yet. And Harris had already been planning on calling David again, albeit not about the case, but still, he was going to make a call, and that was what Harris had promised.

Harris decided he had done the right thing. He didn't want to risk getting David in trouble. And the model number wouldn't even play all that much into the case.

Harris pulled into the driveway and gratefully walked back into his parents' house. It was after 2200, but Harris could still smell his mom's buffalo chicken tater-tot casserole. There was no mistaking it. His dad was asleep on the couch again, but his mom was still up. The TV was once again playing the show about the author who seemed to always solve murders. As soon as Harris walked in, his mother jumped up, looked at the television, and then at Harris.

"Oh honey, I'm so sorry," Petunia said quickly. She reached for the remote to turn the show off. "That's probably in bad taste to be watching this after the last several days."

"No, that's fine, Mom," Harris said quickly. "Maybe it will give me an idea for the case." Harris laughed. No matter how unrealistic the show was, given this one woman seemed to solve dozens of murders, Harris had to admit it was quite a good show.

"In that case, let me catch you up," Petunia said excitedly. "So far, she's found two bodies. One of them falls from a horse and dies, and later his daughter is murdered as well. The only suspect so far is the family dog." Harris looked at his mother, confused. A dog as a murder suspect—that's a stretch.

Petunia continued, "Oh, also, there's some buffalo casserole in the oven for you. I left it on warm. There is either ranch or blue cheese in the fridge. I made the chicken extra spicy this time."

Harris smiled. He loved when his mom made it extra spicy. Harris helped himself to a significant portion and then covered it in ranch. Then he joined his mom on the couch to finish the episode. Before the episode was even over, Harris found his eyelids drooping and, soon after, fell asleep on the couch.

Thursday Morning

Harris woke up to the sound of his phone ringing. He sat up and found a thick afghan on his lap. His mom had clearly covered him up after he fell asleep. He smiled.

Harris looked down at his phone, and it took him a moment to decipher the blurry letters on the screen. He blinked a few times to remove the sleep from his eyes and then realized it was Gonzales calling him. Harris looked at the time, worried he had overslept somehow, but saw that it was before 0600.

Harris swiped to answer, "Why are you waking me up, Gonzales? Are you ok?"

"It happened again," was the reply.

"What did? What happened?" Harris suddenly felt significantly more awake.

"Another body… and I'm the one who found it. I already called it in, but… I…"

Harris could hear the emotion and stress in his partner's voice. After two years as partners, he could decipher the slightest quiver in Gonzales's voice. "I'll be right there. Text me the address."

Harris hung up, hurried to put on a pair of jeans and a solid-colored t-shirt, and quickly laced up his boots. He loaded his bag, grabbed his badge and gun, then left a note on the counter for his parents, who were both still asleep. Running out to his car, he then navigated to the address Gonzales had sent him, driving as fast as humanly possible.

Half an hour later, he arrived at the scene, finding it already media-laden and swarming with officers. Harris saw Gonzales in the crowd, who was beckoning him over. Harris fought his way through the reporters, flashing his badge at the officer guarding the barricade, allowing him to be let through. Making his way to Gonzales, he saw that most of the officers were huddled in an alley.

"What happened, Gonzales?" Harris asked his partner.

"Well, the movie last night ran longer than we expected, so I decided to stay the night at Lucy's. I'd had a couple beers and didn't think it'd be smart to drive. I slept on her couch and got up early this morning because I knew I better get home to take Buster out." Buster was Gonzales's pet bulldog.

"So I was leaving her building this morning," Gonzales pointed to an apartment a few stories up, next to the alley. "I had decided to take the trash out for Lucy, and as I went down the alley to the dumpster, I saw someone lying there. Another body. They were just lying there on their stomach. I dropped the trash bag, I tried feeling for a pulse, but it was too late. They were already cold. That's when I called it in, and then I called you."

Harris led Gonzales farther from the scene and tried his best to comfort him.

But all Harris could think was that there had been two deaths in three days.

Halistad heard the ring of his phone. He was already up eating his bowl of oatmeal while drinking a glass of orange juice. He looked down and saw that it was dispatch calling him.

"Uh-huh," he said into the phone. He listened to the female on the other end. "I'll be right there."

He methodically changed from his robe into slacks, and a blazer, then drove his car to the designated apartment building. He bypassed the media and went directly to the alley. A crime scene investigator was already there, photographing the body and marking evidence. Halistad stepped over a trash bag that was marked with an evidence tag reading '2.'

"What's been done so far?" Halistad barked at one of the deputies.

"Not much, sir. We took an official statement from Deputy Gonzales."

"Why him?" Halistad asked.

"Gonzales called it in. He's the one that found the body," Halistad nodded for the deputy to continue.

The deputy pointed to a dumpster, and next to it was an evidence tag marked '4.' "We found a hypodermic needle partially under a dumpster, and a slight puncture wound on the victim's left arm. We are waiting for a coroner, but we're guessing cyanide poisoning based on the body and its signs. There is a slight aroma of almonds, and the victim's fingernails are blue. We expect a test will confirm cyanide in the needle."

"Any identity yet?" Halistad asked, who was peering down, looking at the victim's face.

"None as of yet, sir. We have him down as a John Doe. We have a deputy checking for any missing person reports, but nothing has turned up yet."

"No form of ID on the body?" Halistad reached down and felt the victim's pockets.

"No, sir, we would say the motive could be robbery since the victim is fully dressed in professional attire but isn't carrying an I.D., keys, or wallet. However, if it is a syringe of cyanide, that may be premeditated."

Halistad stood up and turned to the deputy, "Good work, Deputy. Let me know when the final results come in."

"Yes, sir, I'll get them to you immediately."

Halistad nodded his head and left the scene.

Harris had managed to calm Gonzales down. It was decided he'd take the day off from patrol.

Harris was given the opportunity for a temporary partner, but he told dispatch he could handle the shift alone.

"As long as there are no more murders," he said, wishing it came off as more of a joke than it did. On his way to the station, Harris called David. "What's up, man?" David asked.

"A lot, but this is a non-business call. What's your schedule like this weekend? We need to hang out. It's been way too long."

"Hey, I agree. The weekend is kind of hectic. Sally has a dance recital Saturday, and Nick has a baseball game Sunday." Nick was David's traditional child, and Sally was one of the P.S. kids. They also had a three-month-old named Davey. "I'm wide open Monday, though. Millie's already watching the kids."

"Sounds like a plan. Wanna' hit the bowling alley? We haven't been there since high school."

"Awesome, I'm looking forward to it." David paused for a moment. "Anything else with the murder?"

"Well, kind of. But this is all still extremely off the record. There was another murder."

"What! Alright. Do you need another model number? I can get my laptop right now."

Harris heard rusting and clanking over the line and heard David walking.

"We don't even have a name yet. But thanks. Once we get more, I'll let you know if I need something. Any update on that first request, though? The detective is kind of hounding me for it, but I told him I didn't know anything."

"Should be soon. I discovered that with that password, I can do a lot of things. View old requests, rearrange the order of importance, and view a whole bunch of classified documents. Did you know that a bunch of the original people Kolifax used to create our models actually live in Politopia? Apparently, part of their deal was they donated their DNA and then got to live here anonymously."

"Interesting. Anyone in particular?" Harris asked.

"Those files are double encrypted behind a major firewall, but I'm actually seeing if I can get past it. Its protection is similar to the one used in *Hack-Nation.*"

"Another video game?" Harris asked, laughing.

"Yeah. Who would have thought that the starting quarterback and his best friend, the valedictorian, would lie to detectives and hack into government documents?" David joked. When Harris didn't laugh, David quickly said, "Whoa, dude, I totally didn't mean to put a damper on everything. I don't think you're doing anything wrong. I mean, if we solve a murder, the end justifies the means, right?"

"Yeah. Right," Harris replied half-heartedly. "Look, my shift is about to start. I gotta run. I'll see ya' Monday."

"Alright. Monday. Sorry dude," David said apolo-getically. "Let me know what you need."

"No worries. Will do," Harris said.

Thursday Evening

The joke David had made didn't sit well with Harris. The guilt that he was sworn to uphold the law was gnawing at him, and he was starting to doubt that he was doing the right thing… he was once again debating if he should call Halistad and come clean when he got an email notification. He saw a file attached and opened it. It was the report on James McGrundy's model number. Number 353, just as David had told him. Harris instantly forwarded the message to Halistad after removing David's email from the chain. Harris instantly felt better that he was no longer holding back information.

Seconds after the email came through, Harris got a text from David. *Sorry again. I got that file moved up the list for you. No need for secrets now.*

Harris responded: *Really, no worries, I just want to make sure I'm doing the right thing here.*

David wrote back: *You are, see you Monday.*

Harris started his shift and was relieved it went by with no drama. No more murders, no calls whatsoever. Actually, it was a quiet shift. Most of the time, he spent lost in his own thoughts. Had he really been doing the right thing, not telling Halistad the number as soon as he had learned it? Friend loyalty mattered, but did it matter more than his job? But what about David's job? It also mattered. Did he even really need to be worrying about this at all anymore?

After all, the official report was in, so there were no concerns anymore as everyone had the same information. Harris pushed all his doubts from his mind and forced himself to focus on driving.

He needed to keep murders and model numbers out of his mind. He was driving. Driving the car. That was it. Driving and drinking a hot coffee.

Halistad was sitting at his desk, reviewing the two active homicide cases at the same time. One a stabbing, the other a poisoning.

"Was there an obvious connection?" He pondered to himself, "Who's going to be the one to find it?"

Halistad had been searching through the database, searching to see if there was a way to get an identification for the newest victim, but he had yet to find anything. He was just about to leave for the day when he received an email alert.

He opened it and saw that it had come from Harris. It was the report he had been waiting for. Double-clicking the file, he read the report. "Model 353," he said to himself. With that, he shut down his desktop and left the office, planning to get an early start the next day.

After Harris's shift ended, he stopped by Gonzales's place before heading back to his parents. Harris knocked on the door and instantly heard Buster begin to bark. He heard Gonzales shush him several times before the door unlocked. Gonzales cracked the door open. When he saw that it was Harris, he pulled the door open and invited him in.

"Hey, Harris. What are you doing here?" Gonzales was trying to get Buster to stop jumping up on Harris—without much success.

"Well, I saw how shaken up you were this morning, and I wanted to make sure that you were alright." Harris began to scratch behind Buster's ears, who promptly rolled over so that Harris could rub his belly.

"I think I'm doing fine. I just never really thought I'd be the one to find a body. Well, actually, I never thought I'd even *see* a dead body like that. You want a beer?" Gonzales walked to his fridge and opened it. Harris saw several take-out containers and beer: both canned and bottled.

Harris shook his head, "I've still got to drive home." Harris sat down on the couch, and Buster climbed in his lap. Harris obliged him and continued to scratch his ears.

Gonzales shrugged and grabbed a single can of beer out, popping it open for himself and taking a large swig of it. "Really, thanks for checking in on me. But I'm fine. Seriously rethinking my life choices, but I'm fine. Lucy promised she'd come over tomorrow, and she said she's going to bring over some casseroles." He paused to take another long drink. "So, did they get a model number for the first guy yet?"

"Yeah, actually, they did. Turns out he's a Model 353. Apparently, he used to be a hockey player but had to retire from injuries."

"Huh, well, at least we've got an answer. Any suspects yet?" Gonzales asked.

"None as of yet. My mom knew his parents, so I'm hoping to find something about his past, but we don't know anything for sure."

Gonzales looked at Harris with concern, "Why are you looking into things? That's Halistad's job."

"Yeah, I don't know. It's a sort of like grisly fascination. I can't really explain it, but there is something about all this that fascinates me."

"Wow. You and I have very different mindsets about all of this." Gonzales chuckled.

"Yeah, I suppose we do."

"Anything about the… uh… well, the second body? Has anyone identified them yet?"

"Nothing. So far, he's been labeled a John Doe. Do you mind if I bounce a few things off you?" Harris asked.

When Gonzales nodded his head, Harris continued, "I find it odd that Politopia has gone over two decades without any murders, and suddenly we have two. I feel as though there has to be a connection between the two, but it doesn't quite make sense. A stabbing and poisoning. I don't get it. And I don't know if there's a connection between Jimmy and this John Doe."

Gonzales thought for a moment, "Yeah, I don't know. Maybe there was something connecting their pasts? Maybe talk to some people who knew Jimmy and see if they might recognize the other body? Speaking of talking to people, Lucy told me that last night, around 0200, she had looked out the window because she saw what looked like a flashlight outside. She looked out the window just in time to see a figure moving around the corner of the building. She thought nothing of it at the time, but later, when she heard about the murder, she thought it might have been the suspect."

Harris pulled out his phone and used his password to view the case files. He went to the coroner's report for John Doe and discovered that the coroner had placed the time of death between 0100 and 0300. Lucy's sighting could be a possible clue.

"That matches the report," Harris told Gonzales. "Has she given an official statement yet? This may be our only lead."

"Not yet, she had to work all day today, but she told me she'd do it first thing tomorrow."

"Good, because I can't deal with any more off-the-record information," Harris muttered partially to himself.

"What do you mean?" Gonzales asked after taking another sip of his beer.

"Uh, nothing. I've got to get going, but let me know if you need anything." Harris went to the door to leave as Gonzales went to get another beer and a Chinese takeout container from the fridge.

"Will do. Thanks again for checking up on me."

Harris drove home and once more found his dad asleep on the couch, and his mom was up watching murder mysteries. Today Harris saw a barbeque potato oven bake on the stove, another of his favorite meals.

When Harris came in, he heard his mom call, "Help yourself to as much as you want. Sour cream is on the top shelf. A new episode just started. I'll pause it to wait for you."

"Thanks, Mom," he said back and served himself dinner. He joined his mom on the couch, and she pressed play. He was greeted with the jaunty, upbeat theme song as the amateur sleuth was shown in perilous situations.

Harris didn't see how the woman was able to solve these murders from the most insignificant clue.

The most benign thing seemed to be all that she needed in order to solve the most complicated of cases.

"Why can't I do that?" Harris said aloud.

"What was that, honey?" Petunia asked.

"Oh, just thinking that I wish I could do the same thing she is."

"Sure you can. You just have never had to do something like this before. Speaking of which, I had that bridge game with Jamie. Obviously, losing her son so recently was still really hard for her. But she did tell me that she could meet you for a very short amount of time tomorrow if you'd like. They have to begin preparing for the funeral starting at noon, so any time before that, you can feel free to stop by their house.

His mom reached over to the end table and wrote an address down. She handed the paper to Harris and said, "Here's her address. By the way, I was thinking. You asked if anyone might have a grudge against him. I did remember that there was another kid on his hockey team. They both wanted to be center. Apparently, that is a coveted position in hockey. Kind of like a quarterback in football. The other player had more years of experience, but Jimmy beat him out. I don't know if that's a motive for murder, but it's all I could think of."

"No, that's really good, Mom. Thanks. I appreciate the help. Look, I'm going to go do a little bit of research about that second body and a connection to Jimmy."

"Yes, your father and I had been meaning to ask you about that." Petunia reached over and shook Chuck's leg to wake him up. "Chuck, wake up. Charles is back."

Chuck shook awake and looked around, dazed for a moment. "Yeah, yeah. I'm awake."

Petunia and Chuck looked to Harris expectantly. "Well, I don't really know much about it. There really isn't all that much to know. I would guess that it was premeditated. Cyanide was likely injected into the victim using a hypodermic needle. Gonzales's girlfriend saw a figure leaving the scene around 0200, but that's the only lead we seem to have so far. The needle was wiped of prints. That's all we know." Harris shrugged.

Petunia leaned over and kissed Harris on the forehead. "Good luck," she said.

"Thanks, Mom. I'll see you in the morning."

With that, Harris walked to the office and set up his laptop. He pulled up the search engine and typed in Jimmy's name.

Only a few articles were generated. One of them was an old newspaper about Jimmy's high school team. Connected to it was a photo showing a younger version of Jimmy and two of his teammates in full gear. They had performed the best of any high school in Politopia and then gotten to compete against a non-Politopia team. Not often did people leave Politopia.

Professional sports teams went to compete in tournaments, and Politopia had sent athletes to perform in the Olympics for the first time last year. One of the most influential trips was by Fiona, who performed her songs on a world tour. Harris himself had only left

Politopia once with his high school football team to compete in a tournament, placing second in the Northern Hemisphere.

The other articles were about Jimmy's professional hockey career. His team performed very well and won tournaments pretty consistently. When he played professionally, Jimmy had played on Politopia's team, which was called the Drones. Harris wasn't much of a hockey fan, but he recalled watching a few of their games. His dad enjoyed watching the games, and Harris occasionally watched with him. Once when Harris was around twelve, they went and saw a live game, though that was years before Jimmy's time on the team.

From the articles he found, Harris could see that the Drones had won a few major tournaments. Harris skimmed through a few more articles until he found one talking about Jimmy's career-ending injury.

Apparently, it had been during a game, and Jimmy pulled his Achilles tendon. Major surgery had been required, and the doctor thought it had gone well, but obviously, things turned for the worse, and he had to retire.

Nothing really stood out to Harris as relating particularly to the case, and he didn't see anything about the other player. He'd have to remember to ask Jamie about it when he spoke to her.

For now, he was going to get some sleep, he hadn't gotten more than ten hours of sleep over the last two days, and he was exhausted. Since he didn't start work until the afternoon, Harris would normally sleep in, but now he had this early meeting with Jamie.

Friday Morning

Harris woke up to his alarm early the following day. He wanted to prepare a few things before the meeting. He went back to the office and printed out a few documents from the files to take to his meeting with Jamie. By the time he was done, his mom was awake and making French toast.

The news was playing on the TV. The newscaster was saying, "Another murder has occurred outside an apartment building early yesterday morning.

"We cannot release photos until the victim has been identified and the next of kin informed. It is not known yet whether this case is connected to the prior murder of Jimmy McGrundy.

Harris clicked off the news and ate three slices of his mom's French toast. He told his mom he was leaving and then packed his things for his meeting with Jamie.

He found the address without issue. It was a small duplex. He knocked on the left door, and an older woman answered the door a few moments later. Her eyes were bloodshot, and her hair was tangled.

"Jamie McGrundy?" Harris asked.

"Yes. Charles, right? I don't think I've seen you since you were in middle school. Come on in. I just put on a pot of coffee."

Harris was grateful and followed her in. She led him to a small dining room table, and he sat down.

"Any cream or sugar?" Jamie asked while pouring two mugs of coffee.

"No thanks," he replied. Jamie added a large splash of cream to her mug, along with a heaping spoonful of sugar. She brought the mugs to the table and sat down across from Harris.

"Petunia said you have some questions to ask me about Jimmy. I'd be happy to help in any way possible."

"Let me start by saying I am so sorry for your loss." Jamie smiled weakly at his words and sipped her drink, "Yes. I've been looking into your son's case, trying to determine a suspect of some sort."

"A detective already came by. Halistad, I think his name was? I told him everything I could think might help. But I'm more than willing to tell you too."

"Well, I was speaking with my mom, and she told me there was a small amount of strife between Jimmy and one of the other players. Something about team positions?"

"She must have been talking about Carl. Yes, Carl had been on the team a few years longer than Jimmy, yet Jimmy received the better position. I don't imagine that would lead to murder through. From my understanding, he and Jimmy were on pretty good terms at... well, at the end. I believe that Carl took his position after Jimmy had to retire, but Jimmy was happy for him."

This whole time Harris had been writing in a notebook. "Do you have a last name for Carl?"

Jamie thought for a moment, "I don't recall off the top of my head. I can dig out some old team photos later if you'd like. I can get his name off his jersey."

"I'd appreciate that. Are there any other people that may have held a grudge of any sort against Jimmy?"

"Your mom asked me that, and I have been thinking. I honestly have no idea. Everyone always loved Jimmy. He was always such a good kid. I know people always say that in situations like this, but in Jimmy's case, it was true."

Harris saw a tear forming in the corner of Jamie's eye and could tell that it was time for him to leave. There had been a few more questions that he wanted to ask, like about the John Doe, but he didn't want to cause any more distress for Jamie than she was already in. He finished the last sip of coffee in the mug and said, "Thank you for your time and the coffee. Again, I am so sorry." She smiled slightly again and walked him to the door.

"As soon as I find those photos, I'll send you a copy of them. Is there anything else I can do to help?"

Harris was about to say no when he suddenly had an idea. "Actually, yes, there is. Is there any chance I could get a phone number for Ms. Heelson?"

"Why, of course. Let me write it down for you." She wrote the number and the name 'Gertrude Heelson' on a sticky note and gave it to him. Harris thanked her and handed her a card, telling her where to send the photos. When he got into his car, he drove around the block and pulled over. First, he called his mom.

She answered, "Hey honey, how's Jamie?"

"She seemed to be holding up under the circumstances. I wanted to let you know that I'll be home a little later than planned. I decided to go talk to Gertrude."

"Thanks for letting me know. I figured we'd do leftovers for lunch, so help yourself to anything in the fridge when you get home. Your father and I have some errands to run later, so we might not be home."

"Why don't you just send me a shopping list? I can pick some things up on the way home."

"Are you sure? I don't want to add to your load," Petunia said.

"It's really no problem. I'd be happy to."

"Alright, dear, I'll write that list and send it over to you soon. Love you."

"I love you too, Mom." He hung up and then dialed Gertrude's number.

He was concerned she wouldn't answer, given it was a new number, but she answered after a few rings.

"Hello?"

"Hello. Is this Gertrude Heelson? This is Deputy Harris. We spoke for a few moments the other day. I was hoping you had a few moments to talk."

"I already gave an official statement. I don't know what else I can tell you."

"I understand, but it would only be for a few moments."

"I suppose that would be fine. Are you available right now? I assume you know where my house is," she said.

"Yes, I can be there in ten minutes," Harris said and hung up. Before driving away, he read over the original statements given by Gertrude. "A short figure around 1800…" he read aloud.

Harris then drove directly to Gertrude's house and found Jimmy's house sealed up with security tape on the doors and windows. Harris parked on the street and walked up to Gertrude's door. He knocked once and waited for Gertrude to answer. She opened the door and ushered Harris in.

Her hostess skills were not as welcoming as Jamie's. "What did you need to ask?" she said.

"I was just hoping you could tell me what exactly happened the other night."

"I already told this all to the deputy that night, but alright," Harris could tell that she didn't wish to relay what she had seen again. "I was just sitting down for my soap opera, *Hopes for Yesterday*. It was a special episode. Tiffany was about to admit that she was the one married to Rodney, not Britney. Anyways, I had just sat down when I looked out the window and saw this tall, heavy-set figure leaving Jimmy's house. They looked to be wearing a trench coat. I figured he was just having a friend over, but then I got this strange feeling, so I called Jimmy. I called him a couple of times, but he never answered. Eventually, I decided to check on him. I found the door unlocked and partially open. I thought that he had forgotten to lock up on his way out. I rationalized and told myself that the figure I saw leaving had been Jimmy. I was just about to lock the door when I saw the body. Like I said, I already told all this to that other deputy. Gonzales was his name. Decent fellow, I suppose. I don't see why I have to talk to you now as well."

"I understand, ma'am. I appreciate your time. I apologize that this is the third time you've had to retell what you saw."

Gertrude looked confused. "Third time?" she asked.

Harris, also feeling confused now, said, "Right, you've spoken with Deputy Gonzales and Detective Halistad. Now you're retelling the story to me."

"I've only spoken to Deputy Gonzales and now you today. I'm not sure who Detective Hallie Stood, or whatever you said his name was, is. I hope this doesn't mean he is going to come to bother me too." Gertrude sounded angry at the thought of having to tell the story again. Harris wondered if this gruff mannerism was a defense mechanism from the pain of losing Jimmy. From how it sounded, Gertrude had been very close to Jimmy, and she must be hurting.

Harris tried to hide the confusion he was feeling.

"Oh, right. Sorry. Well, if by any chance you do remember anything else, please give me a call."

"I will, but I don't image I'll remember much," Gertrude replied somewhat rudely. The disgust she had, having to relay this information again, was very prevalent in her mannerisms and tone.

Harris left and walked past Jimmy's house. It looked so serene, almost too much so, given the recent murder that had occurred. Harris looked back and saw that Gertrude was peering past a curtain at him. He hurried to his car and drove away. He pulled to the local market and looked at the grocery list his mom had sent him.

From the ingredients, he surmised that she intended to make some sort of Asian stir-fry tonight. He went through the store gathering all the items and decided to pick up some things to make Piña Colada cupcakes at the last minute. He didn't bake very often, but he loved making these during the summer.

They were bright, fruity, not overly sweet, and perfect for eating by the pool. He also picked up a few essential items, thinking that if he were going to stay with his parents for at least a few days, he would help out with meals.

He knew his mom would insist on doing all the cooking, but that didn't mean he couldn't at least purchase the food.

He finished the shopping and headed home. His dad was sitting at the table playing solitaire, and his mom was folding laundry on the couch.

"Hey, Mom. Hey, Dad. I got all the items on your list. And I also got ingredients to make cupcakes."

"That's so nice, sweetie. Thank you."

His dad did a fist pump. His usual sign of approval that Harris was making one of his favorite desserts.

Harris found leftover mac-and-cheese in the fridge and heated it in the microwave. He added hot sauce to the top and told his parents, "I'm going to write up these reports."

Harris returned to the office and began typing up his notes one-handed while enjoying the mac-and-cheese. When he was done, he realized something hadn't made sense from Gertrude's interview. He thought he remembered reading something different in her statement than what she said today. He pulled up the original statement Gonzales had taken to compare facts. He was scanning through the facts when he noticed one inconsistency. "Tall and heavy set… short… That's odd. Gertrude described the figure differently each time. She must not be a very reliable witness."

Harris finished filing the reports when he got a message on his phone. It was from Jamie: *I found those old photos. I sent a few of them. Jimmy was number 8, and Carl was in jersey 15. His last name was Gilmore. Let me know if you need anything else.*

Harris wrote back to her. *Thank you, you've been a big help.*

Harris didn't want to add Carl Gilmore as a suspect yet. He felt the need to talk to him first before making anything definite. However, he added Carl Gilmore's name as a person of interest. Even if he wasn't a suspect, he might be able to lead to a suspect. He also made sure to add Jamie's interview to the files.

Halistad got another alert on his phone. More documents had been filed under the McGrundy case. They seemed to be duplicates of what had already been filed from the initial interview with McGrundy's neighbor and with Jamie McGrundy. He opened the interview with Jamie and scanned through it. It was all the same information for the most part. There was one new piece of information, though—a note about Carl Gilmore, who had a potential grudge against Jimmy.

Halistad made a note of that and then opened the other file. It was another interview with the neighbor. He noticed one thing that seemed to be a discrepancy, "Tall and heavy-set figure?"

He opened the original interview and read, "Short figure. That's odd," Halistad said grumpily.

Halistad made a note on a piece of paper, closed out of the files, and shut down his desktop. It was only the afternoon, but Halistad was already exhausted. He didn't realize dealing with murder could be so exhausting.

Friday Night

Harris waited for his mom to get dinner started, and when she cleared out, he took over in the kitchen. He had just finished baking his cupcakes and had a mountain of dishes to clean.

Harris cleaned the dishes, then frosted the cupcakes. He topped each one with half of a maraschino cherry and a little paper umbrella. He placed several on a platter he found in the cupboard. He went out back to meet his parents at the pool. Harris had loved growing up with a pool in the backyard. He was always able to throw the best parties for all of his friends.

Harris placed the platter of Piña Colada cupcakes on a small table near the lounge chairs, took off his shirt, and laid out on a lounge chair to sunbathe. He had already switched into swim trunks before baking. It was a good thing his mom was always prepared because she already had ample clothes for him in the dresser, including the pair of green Hawaiian print trunks he was wearing now.

"Dessert is served," he said.

"Before dinner? Didn't your parents raise you better than that?" Chuck laughed.

"Nope," Harris replied with a chuckle.

Each of them took a cupcake and quickly devoured them.

"How do you get such a rich pineapple taste, Charles? These are always fantastic."

His mom had been wanting to add the recipe to her cookbook for a long time, but Harris said that bakers didn't reveal their secrets. Harris finally gave in and told her. "I substitute the milk for pineapple juice and then add crushed pineapple right in the batter."

"Genius," she replied. Harris reached for another cupcake. He figured he'd swim a couple extra laps in the pool tonight to burn off the calories. Harris laid out for nearly half an hour when they all heard a ding from inside.

"Brown rice is ready!" Petunia called and hurried inside. She came back a few minutes later with a serving tray and three large bowls. Also on the tray was a bottle of soy sauce and a bottle of sriracha.

"Poolside service? This must be a five-star resort." Harris said, taking a bowl from his mom. He added a healthy squeeze of sriracha and a small splash of soy sauce. His mom had already seasoned the chicken and vegetables enough that he didn't need to add much.

The family enjoyed a pleasant meal outdoors under the setting sun, talking about anything and everything except the homicide cases.

When they finished, Petunia insisted on doing the dishes again, and Harris stayed outside to absorb the last few rays of the sun. Once the sun had set, he turned on the pool lights and started swimming his laps. He hadn't swum in quite a while but had done some competitive swimming in high school and had been on a community water polo team, so it came back quickly. Within a few minutes, he was completing kick turns and switching seamlessly between back, breast, butterfly, and freestyle strokes.

Harris swam for about forty-five minutes and then went inside to shower. After a good hot shower, he went back to the living room to sit with his mom. She had finished up the dishes and was working on the blanket she was knitting.

"So, how did it go with Jamie? Anything helpful?" Harris's mom already had two more of the cupcakes on a plate offering one to Harris.

"Oh yeah, I'd almost forgotten. Jamie got me the name of that teammate, but she doesn't think there's a connection. She also sent me some old team photos." Harris held a cupcake in one hand while pulling out his phone with the other.

He opened the email to view the photos. He held his phone out to his mom, so he could share the pictures with her. The first picture was of a cut-out from a magazine clipping Harris had already seen from Jimmy's high school days. There were a couple photos from games, one of which showed Carl turned around, about to take a shot.

You could read '15' and 'Gilmore' across his back. It seemed that Carl had played on Jimmy's team both in high school and when they were on the Drones. The final photo was a team shot, showing the players kneeling on the ice and a coach standing behind them. It was from Jimmy's high school yearbook.

"Oh, look at Jimmy," Petunia said. "He looked so happy and full of life. I just can't imagine anyone having a reason to murder him."

"It certainly is strange," Harris muttered. He felt there was something he was missing. He had a feeling the answer must be right in front of him. Then he saw it. The goalie, jersey number 23. "Mom. Come with me."

Harris set his cupcake down on the coffee table and hurried down the hall to the office. His mom was only a step behind him.

Harris booted up his laptop and quickly navigated through the case files. He found the picture he was looking for and printed it out. Next, he opened up the team photo, zoomed in on player number 23, and pressed print again. Once he had them side by side, he held them out to his mom.

"Is it just me, or are these the same people?" Harris asked her.

She took a moment to look at the photos and then nodded her head, "I'd have to say so. The nose, jaw, and eye structures are identical. Who is this?" She looked up at Harris. "Do you think he's a suspect?"

He pointed to the computer screen and clicked a few keys, and there popped up the same photo.

The top of the screen read 'Doe, John. Homicide. Cyanide Poisoning.'

"No, Mom. This man is dead. We just found our John Doe," Harris said. "Let's see if we can find a name for him."

With his mom's help, Harris searched through the other photos, hoping one of them showed the back of number 23's jersey to attain the last name, but unfortunately, none did.

"Mom, do you think Jamie would still be awake?"

Petunia looked at the wall clock. 2312. "She could be, but I'm not sure. You need to give her a call?"

"Yes." Harris pulled out his phone and clicked on Jamie's number. The phone rang several times. Harris was about to hang up when Jamie answered. "Mrs. McGrundy. This is Deputy Harris again. I need to ask you a question."

Jamie yawned. Harris felt a moment of guilt, realizing he had woken her up. "Call me Jamie, and what do you need?" She didn't sound upset, fortunately.

"Do you know who wore jersey number 23 when Jimmy played in high school?"

"Not off the top of my head. Let me see if it's in any of the photos." She replied.

"I already checked the ones you sent me."

"I have a few others that I didn't send. They didn't have Jimmy or Carl in them, so I didn't think you'd need them. One moment so I can check the others."

Harris heard the bed creak, and a man's voice said something, then Jamie responded, "It's alright, honey. Yes, everything's fine. Go back to sleep."

Talking to Harris now, she said, "Let me call you back in a few minutes." The phone hung up, and all Harris could do was wait.

It was the longest three minutes of Harris's life, but finally, Jamie called back. "I'm sorry, but I couldn't find a full name. It looks like it starts with R-O-S, but that's all I can make out. Sorry I couldn't have been more helpful. I'll send that photo over to you now."

"That is more than helpful. Thank you so much. I am sorry for waking you, though." Harris said with equal parts guilt for waking her and encouragement that he may have just found a huge piece of the puzzle.

"It's no problem. Make sure to get some rest." Jamie said in that special tone only mothers seem to have.

Harris ended the call and then turned to his mom. "We have part of a name. R-O-S. But I'll need more than that to make anything official."

"Where do we go from here, then?" Harris heard the energy in her voice.

"*We*. What do you mean we?" Harris asked. He didn't know how he felt about his mom investigating a murder.

"We're in this together now. Let me help any way I can."

"I suppose I could try contacting the High School Hockey League. They may still have it in their records what their player's numbers were. I doubt anyone would answer the phone right now, though."

"We'll take care of that first thing in the morning, then. For now, let's get some rest."

Saturday Morning

Harris's mom woke him early the following day. "Charles, you ready to make that call?"

"Mom! What time is it?" He squinted at the window. He couldn't even see any light coming through yet.

"It's just before six o'clock in the morning. You'll want to make that call before practice starts."

"Okay, give me a second." Petunia left the room. Harris yawned and threw on a pair of shorts and a tank top. He then walked the familiar routine to the hallway, stopping first in the bathroom, then heading to the kitchen. He was just about to put his hand on the handle of the coffee pot when his mom called out, "I poured you a cup of coffee, son." Harris shook his head and smiled, continuing the path to meet his mom in the living room. She was sitting on the couch with two cups of coffee. Harris sat beside her and took a sip of the hot coffee.

"Thanks, Mom."

"Always," she replied like she always did. Then she playfully punched him on the arm, also like she always did.

After a quick search, he found the phone number to call.

"How may I direct your call?" the voice on the phone said. It sounded like a younger guy, probably a college student getting internship hours.

"Hi, my name is Deputy Charles Harris Jr. I needed to get some information about a former player's name."

"I'm very sorry, sir, we aren't at liberty to disclose information like that. There is a form online, however, that you can file to request that." Harris internally groaned at the idea of more paperwork.

"Are you sure there can't be an exception? This is very important," Harris begged.

"I'm sorry, sir, that's company policy."

"Okay, I understand, thank you," Harris ended the call.

"What did they say," Petunia asked.

"They can't disclose that sort of information."

"Give me the phone," she said and took it before her son answered. She redialed the number and waited for an answer.

"Hi there. I have been trying to track down some information. I'm planning a class reunion for my son, and I need to get the jersey number of one of his teammates." Pause. "Yes, I'm trying to put together care packages for each of them with their old team numbers." Pause. "Well, I don't want to ask because I didn't want to offend him." Pause. "You could do that for me? Oh, you're a lifesaver." Pause. "Name? Well, you see, my son wasn't all that close to him. They always just called him the 'Fridge.'"

Harris stared at his mom with a look of bewilderment. "Yes, he did play goalie. The boys claimed he could block any shot," she laughed. Pause. " Hmmm. I do remember his name started with an R, something like Roswell, maybe?" Pause. "Yes, I'm pretty sure it was an R-O-S something or other." Pause. "Yes! Of course! I remember now! That was his name! You're a lifesaver. What was his jersey number again?" Pause. "23? Perfect. Got it." Pause. "Thanks. Have a great day."

"You got it?" Harris was shocked by how quickly his mom got the information.

"Yup. Never doubt the power of a mom. Especially when someone thinks she's a frantic mom."

Harris nodded his head in approval and said, "So, what's his name?"

"Henry Rosburg. Played goalie, jersey number 23."

"You're fantastic, Mom. I have to update the case file now," Harris hurried back to the office to begin adding this newfound information to the report. 'John Doe, possible identity, Henry Rosburg. Model number pending.'

As soon as he was done updating that, he made another call. It was sent to voicemail.

A text came through a few seconds later from David. *Can't answer. At daughter's recital. What's up?*

Harris wrote back: *Need model number. When can you talk?*

A message came back: *If it's urgent, I can talk for a few. Sally's not on for 45 min. Currently watching 3-year-olds run into each other in tutus. I'll take any excuse to get out.*

Harris laughed and wrote back: *It's urgent.*

David responded: *All right. Heading to lobby.*

A few moments later, David called Harris back.

"What's up, Charles?"

"I think I've got an identity for the second body. The John Doe was Henry Rosburg, around the same age as Jimmy. It turns out that he and Jimmy played hockey together in high school. I need a model number to add to the report."

"Can do. I can *expedite*," he emphasized the word, making it clear the info wouldn't be official, "things for you tonight after the recital. I'll still need paperwork before anything official is released."

"Understood, and sorry about that freak-out the other day."

"You're fine. You've got a lot on your mind. Are we still on for Monday?" David asked, sounding hopeful.

"Wouldn't miss it. How does 10:00 am sound? I work later that evening."

"I'll see you then. It looks like the 4-year-olds are on. They're doing Swan Lake… kind of. Later."

"Later, man."

Harris uploaded the photos that he had received to the file case, then noticed a new tag had been placed on the McGrundy file. He clicked on it, and two words appeared on the screen, 'Cold Case.'

Harris was shocked. It had been less than a week, and they had already deemed it a cold case? That seemed too soon, especially with the second homicide so shortly afterward. It wasn't yet decided if they were connected.

Halistad had just finished going through the McGrundy file. Based on the evidence and the lack of possibility of witnesses, he had deemed the McGrundy murder to be a cold case. He had just barely added the note when his phone rang.

He barked into the phone, "What?"

"This is Deputy Harris, sir. I wanted to know if you had seen the newest marking on the McGrundy case. It's been marked a cold case."

"Yes, I did, Deputy. I have closed this case. There is a lack of evidence and not enough witnesses."

"Don't you think it's a little soon to be closing the case, sir? It was only a few days ago, and I still had a few interviews pla-"

Halistad interrupted, "You! If I remember correctly, Deputy Harris, you are a street cop, not a detective. I'll ask that you leave the investigations to me. Am I understood?"

"You have made your point clear, sir," Harris said sharply.

"Good, now I've got work to do. Goodbye." Halistad ended the call before waiting for a response.

Harris didn't care what Halistad had said. There were too many unanswered questions in the case. Harris felt it irresponsible to close the case so soon. He couldn't let a murder like this go unsolved.

He went out to the kitchen and found his mom mopping the floor.

"Mom, do you mind if I talk to you for a minute?"

"Of course, honey. What's going on?" She leaned the mop on the wall and sat down at the table with Harris.

"Well, I just got off the phone with Detective Halistad. He's already called the homicide a cold case."

"This soon?"

"Yeah, that's what I thought. I feel like there is still a lot to learn about this case, and, well… I know it wasn't really my case, but I still feel like I should work on it, even if it's unofficially. Do you think that's the right thing to do?"

"I trust your judgment, son. If you think there's more to learn from this case, then I agree. I just want you to promise you'll keep your father and me in the loop."

"I will, Mom. Okay, I have to get ready for work now. I have to stop by my apartment. I need to get my bowling gear. David and I are going bowling on Monday."

"David, David Jenson? It's been ages since you've seen him. Since when did you start talking?"

"He's been helping me on the case, all unofficial."

"I'm so glad to hear that. He was a very good friend," she said. "How is he?"

"He seems to be doing fine. He's at his daughter's dance recital right now."

"That's sweet. Well, I better get back to mopping, and you have to leave for work. I'll see you tonight. Any dinner requests?"

"Surprise me. Everything you make is great," Harris replied happily.

Harris packed up and drove to his apartment, parking in his reserved spot. Punching in his passcode at the door, he headed up the three flights of stairs to his apartment.

He started to unlock his door when his neighbor, Ms. Guiness, opened her door.

"Oh, Charles, I was hoping it was you. I've been waiting to give this to you."

She disappeared back into her apartment for a moment, then reappeared holding a package.

"A delivery came for you today. I told the delivery man that he could just leave it with me. I hope that's alright. I noticed you hadn't been here for a few days. If you hadn't come back by tomorrow, I was going to ask the landlord for your phone number, but now here you are!" She laughed and smiled as she handed over the box.

"That's just fine, Ms. Guiness. Thank you." He took the package from her.

"The delivery man said it was marked as important and that you needed to open it as soon as possible," she said before disappearing back into her apartment.

Harris unlocked his door and went into his apartment. He placed the package on the counter and began to gather his things. He grabbed his bowling gear, then packed up a backpack with a few more changes of clothes. He had been enjoying staying with his parents and planned on doing so for at least the next several days.

Harris still had an hour before work started, so he thought he would tidy up a bit. He vacuumed his apartment and washed some dishes that he realized he had left in the sink. When he had left for work the other day, the day of the first murder that had started all of this, he had still been planning on coming back to his home at the end of the day.

He was just about to leave when he remembered the package.

He looked at the label and saw it was addressed to him. However, Harris didn't recognize the return address. Grabbing a knife from a kitchen drawer, he slit the tape and pulled the flaps up.

He heard a click… and it all happened in the blink of an eye… he felt every instinct in his body telling him to hit the floor, and he did, just as the package exploded.

Saturday Evening

Harris didn't know what happened for the next several minutes, but the next thing he knew, he was being shaken awake by someone. He couldn't open his eyes, but he could hear someone calling his name. His right arm was in pain, and he could feel something warm dripping down his cheek.

"Harris! Come on, man. Wake up! Charles!" Harris groaned in response. "What happened? Are you okay?"

Harris was able to recognize the voice was Gonzales. Harris was finally able to force his eyes open, but everything was blurry. He sat up, trying to look at his partner.

"Huh… it was, um…" Charles felt groggy, and it took a moment for his thoughts to clear enough to formulate words. "The uh, the package exploded. Why are you here?"

"I was on my way to work, listening to the police scanner when I heard the call about the explosion. One of your neighbors called it in. I recognized the address and drove here as fast as I could. I knew the bomb squad would take several minutes to get here. Fortunately, I was just around the corner. The main door was locked, but I flashed my badge, and one of your neighbors let me in. I had to break your door. Sorry."

Harris sat up now and looked around. He saw a massive black burn and a melted section of the cheap plastic counter. Black char marks were on the cupboards as well as the walls around them. Part of the ceiling had cracked and fallen to the ground, leaving a blanket of white dust on the carpet. He looked at his front door and saw it was swinging open on partially broken hinges.

"That's fine. I... I... think I'm okay." Harris tried to stand up, pushing himself up on his right arm. He instantly winced and collapsed.

"You alright?" Gonzales asked.

"I don't know. My arm hurts really bad. I think it may be broken." He reached over with his left hand and carefully felt down his right arm. A few inches above his wrist made him hiss in pain. "Definitely broken. Help me up, would you?" Harris could hear sirens in the parking lot below.

Gonzales reached down, putting one hand under Harris's right armpit, the other on his left side, helping him to stand up slowly. Gonzales reached into his back pocket and pulled out a green bandana. He fashioned a sling out of it for Harris's broken arm. "You good to walk, man?"

"Yeah, I think so. Can you grab those bags, though?" Harris pointed to his backpack and the bowling bag.

EMTs and police arrived at this point and came through the already broken door. Two cops had made entry into the apartment with their guns drawn and at the ready. Gonzales showed them his badge, while Harris used his left hand to provide his badge as well.

"Deputy Gonzales," Gonzales stated, placing his hand on his chest to introduce himself, "and this is Deputy Harris," gesturing to Harris. "His arm is broken, among other injuries, and needs to be taken care of. I can take him to the hospital."

The cops let them pass. The partners made their way down the stairs very slowly together. Harris still felt incredibly groggy. He had never experienced the amount of pain he was in. Gonzales helped Harris into the passenger side seat of his car, carefully guiding the seat belt to maneuver around Harris's broken arm. While that all had taken quite a bit of slow going and patience, Gonzales didn't hesitate to drive well over the speed limit. Pulling up to the emergency hospital within five minutes.

As they entered into the hospital, Gonzales held up his badge. Looking right into the eyes of the nurse that was sitting at the admittance desk, he stated, "I'm Deputy Gonzales. This is my partner Deputy Harris. He was injured in an explosion. He needs help, now."

If Harris hadn't been in throbbing pain from the top of his head to the bottom of his feet, he would have congratulated Gonzales for taking charge, proving that his model number didn't dictate his true ability to be a hero. The nurse nodded her head, understanding the urgency in his voice, and immediately stood up, while simultaneously pressing the large button that swung open the two large doors that allowed access back to the emergency room.

Gonzales stayed with Harris and continued to say encouraging things, as well as, "Come on, tough guy." Even when the nurse tried to send Gonzales to the waiting room, he refused and stayed with Harris.

Moving around them, the nurse began working quickly to get Harris out of his clothes and into a hospital gown.

An hour later, Harris had received several X-rays and a plaster cast and had been well-checked for a concussion.

The final verdict was that he had indeed broken his arm in two places. Both fractures were mild. The doctor saw no reason that the bones wouldn't mend nicely while in the cast, doubting there would be any permanent injury. Harris also had signs of a very mild concussion.

The doctor assured him that there would be no lasting brain damage and that most of his symptoms would likely be relieved by later that evening.

The only other injuries he had sustained were scratches and burns on his face and arms from shrapnel. These were easily cleaned and soothed by the antiseptic and bandages used to address them.

Once Harris received the all-clear to be discharged, he changed back into his clothes, and he and Gonzales made their way back out of the hospital to the car. When Harris had been taken back to get the imaging done, Gonzales had run out to move the car away from the front of the hospital and into an actual parking spot.

As they walked a bit to get to the car's new spot, Gonzales asked, "Do you want me to go get the car? You can wait here."

Harris sighed and said, "It actually feels good to walk and stretch a little bit after all that."

Gonzales laughed, "I'm just glad you're walking, man. You scared me for a minute there when I was trying to wake you up in your apartment."

"Thanks for being there." Harris didn't need quite so much fussing getting situated into the car this time around. They still took a few extra minutes to get the seat belt around the cast, with Gonzales doing the buckling as Harris learned how to manage his arm in a cast.

Once settled, Harris checked his phone. He winced as the bright light from the screen hurt his eyes, a symptom of his concussion. He dimmed the screen and then was able to see he had several missed calls from his parents. He quickly called them back.

His mom answered before the first ring had even finished. "Oh, honey! Are you alright? Where are you? We saw on the news that there was an explosion at your building." His mom paused, but before Harris could respond and assure her he was okay, she was calling out, "Chuck! Get in here! It's Charles." Her voice came back to the phone. "They didn't report if there were any casualties or who was injured. Oh, we have been so worried. Are you alright?"

"Mom… Mom! Take a deep breath, Mom." Harris interrupted her questions with a small smile. He knew his mom loved him so much she just couldn't help worrying. "I'm okay, Mom. Stay calm while I tell you what happened. Remember you're talking to me right now, so you know this has a happy ending. I was home. The explosion was actually in my apartment. I don't really know what happened, but the good news is I'm okay. Gonzales heard about the explosion and came to check on me. He found me in the apartment. He woke me up and got me to the hospital. I have a broken arm and a super mild concussion. I'm a little scraped up. But I'm okay."

"Oh, sweetheart! That's awful. Thank God you're okay. You're coming back here, right? Dad and I will help you while you mend. What hospital are you at? Do you need us to come to pick you up? Should I bring you some clean clothes? Have you gotten to eat anything?"

"No, Mom," Harris couldn't help but chuckle at how much his mom was, well, being a mom. "Gonzales is still here with me. He stayed the whole time I was here. He's driving me back to your place now…"

Harris paused as he listened to Petunia's response and question. "Ok, Mom, I'll ask him. Can you ask Dad if he will go with him to get my car when we get there?” Harris looked at Gonzales to make sure this plan was okay.

Gonzales nodded his head. Harris continued, “My car is still at my apartment, and I shouldn’t drive right now.”

“Of course he will, sweetie,” Petunia said. “I love you.”

Chuck’s voice came over the phone, “Let us know if you need anything else. I love you, son.”

“I love you both too. I’ll be home soon.” Harris ended the call and looked at his partner. “So what’s your favorite meal, and also, what’s your favorite kind of cake?”

“Why on earth are you asking me about cake? You were just in an explosion?! Oh, man, is your head worse than they thought? Maybe I should take you back to the hospital for more tests.” Gonzales sounded worried as he questioned Harris. He turned on the car blinker and started to turn around back to the hospital.

Harris started laughing, which only caused his partner to think he had seriously lost it.

“I’m fine. My mom said to ask you and tell you she’s going to make you a hero’s dinner for helping me.” Harris chuckled as he laid his head back against the headrest and closed his eyes.

“Hey, no sleeping!” Gonzales barked at him, “The doc said you can’t sleep for at least a few hours with that concussion. We don’t want any unconsciousness.”

He took a deep breath and then sighed, "You scared me again, man, asking about cake at a time like this. Honestly!"

Gonzales shook his head, relieved his partner was okay. "Don't scare me anymore today. I need a break…and it's tamales, okay? And I like cherry pie more than cake… with ice cream *and* whip cream." Gonzales then joined him in laughing too.

"Alright, that will be a great hero's meal."

Harris pulled out his phone and texted his mom: *Tamales and cherry pie with the works.*

She wrote back: *Got it, tell him thanks again for us.*

Harris thought for a moment and wrote back: *The screen hurts my eyes. Putting phone away. Love you. Be home soon.*

"My folks say thanks again," Harris told Gonzales. Harris leaned his head back again. His eyes hurt from the sun, so he closed his eyes.

Gonzales started to say something, but Harris interrupted him. "And I'm not going to sleep. I was just thinking. Why would someone set a bomb off at my place? Is this a serial killer? Why would I be a target? I don't have any connection to the other cases."

"You know anything else about those two?" Gonzales asked.

"A bit. We got an ID on the John Doe. His name was Henry Rosburg. It appears that he and Jimmy played hockey together in high school. Another player on the team had a bit of an issue with Jimmy, but I don't know anything yet.

"Speaking of which, can you do something for me? I need an address, but even the dimmed screen light is starting to hurt my eyes."

"No problem," Gonzales pulled the car into a mostly deserted parking lot and pulled out his phone. "You have a name?"

"Yeah, Carl Gilmore."

Gonzales logged on and went to the database. He scrolled through and finally found the address. "I got it. Want me to send it to you?"

"No, actually, if you could just drive us there now?" Harris asked, "Then we can head to my parents."

"Are you sure you're okay to go anywhere? Doc made it pretty clear you were supposed to be resting," Gonzales said as he started the car.

"This is murder," Harris said. "I can't let anyone else die, not if I can prevent it."

"I understand," Gonzales replied. He pulled the car onto the road and began following the navigation.

After a few minutes on the road, Harris said, "Obviously, I can't go to work today. Is there any way you could burn a vacation day? I think I'm going to need some help. I'm sorry to ask."

"You don't have to apologize. I'm happy to do it," Gonzales replied quickly.

They both called in: Harris using sick time and Gonzales using vacation time.

Carl's address was still about a half hour away, so Harris decided to make a call, but he had to tell Gonzales something first.

Harris looked at his partner, "Hey, I need to make a call. I have an informant that I've been working with on the case. I'm going to call him and see if he's willing to talk to both of us. If he says yes, I need you to swear to never talk about what he tells us."

"You've got my word," Gonzales said, and Harris believed him.

Harris dialed David's number, then held the phone to his ear. David answered and said, "Hey, you caught me at the perfect time. It's intermission right now."

"We have to talk, but I must tell you first that I'm with my partner Gonzales. I trust him to keep this conversation between the three of us, but it's your call."

"Hang on," David said. Harris heard David in a muffled voice, "Millie, I've got to take this outside. It's business. I'll be back before the finale." Back to Harris, he asked, "You really trust him?"

"Think of him like our old friend Johnny." Harris hoped David got the code. Johnny Mendell had been one of their friends in high school. They'd been close to him but didn't share all their plans with him. Harris trusted Gonzalez, but he didn't want to put his partner in the crossfire if they had to go around the law.

"Ok, I hear you. We can tell some, but not all," David said knowingly.

"Exactly," Harris responded, happy he had understood the message. "So you're willing to talk?"

"Yeah, go ahead and put me on speaker."

Harris did so and then said, "Alright, first an update. Have you seen the news yet?"

"No, I've been at the recital. What happened? Another murder?"

"Well, an attempted murder." Harris could hear David start to form a question, "And before you ask who, it was me. I'm fine, broken arm and concussion. Fortunately, Gonzales was nearby and took me to the hospital. In fact, he got there before the medics. We're heading now to talk with Carl Gilmore, a possible suspect. But my biggest question now is, 'Why?'

"I first thought they were trying to silence me because I may be on to something, but I feel like I haven't figured anything out. And no one really knows what I've been doing, besides you two and my parents, of course. Well, and Jamie, I guess, but I don't see why she would try to kill me. I'm trying to solve her son's murder. There doesn't seem to be any answers yet."

"Dang, dude, I'm glad to hear you're all right. Let's start by going over what we actually know. So Jimmy and Henry were on the team together. Maybe someone's going after the whole team? Possibly a team that lost to them and held a long-term grudge?"

"Could be." Harris said, "Gonzales, do you think you could get a history of scores between Jimmy's team and other teams? Specifically ones that Jimmy's team won by a significant amount."

"Can do. I'll get started on that as soon as I get home," Gonzales said.

"I think we do have to be honest, though," David said, "It's possible that Carl held this grudge longer than we expected. He could very well be the murderer."

Harris looked to Gonzales while saying, "We're checking that out now. We are en route to his house."

"Ah," David said, "right into the possible hornets' nest. Solid plan. I approve. So what do you need from me?"

"Nothing as of now, just those things we'd already talked about."

"I'll have it for you tonight. Do you need them sooner? I can leave now if you need them. I'm sure Millie could record the finale for me. I already saw Sally's solo."

"No, that's fine. I don't want you to miss family time. We're almost to Carl's now. I'll let you know how it goes."

"Hang on. Take me off speaker phone," David said. Harris looked at Gonzales, confused. His partner shrugged in response, and Harris did as David asked.

"Can Gonzales hear me?" David asked. He seemed to be worried about something.

"No. What's up? You find something new?" Harris asked, confused.

"No, I actually had a question for you." David lowered his voice and said, "You said that Gonzales was nearby when the explosion went off? How long did it take for him to get there?" Harris was about to respond when David quickly said, "Just say a number."

Harris thought for a second. He couldn't give an exact number because he wasn't actually sure how long it had been. Then he said, "I don't know how long it took for my computer to turn on. The screen went black for quite a while."

"So you blacked out?" David confirmed.

"Yeah. Why do you need to know?" Harris asked. His eyes flicked to Gonzales, who didn't seem to notice.

"Well, I was thinking. It sounds like Gonzales got there unnaturally fast. To get there before medics is somewhat odd. I may have read too many murder mystery novels, but sometimes the first person to get to the scene is the one who was expecting the murder the most. I may be totally off, but I was thinking that

Gonzales might somehow be connected to all of this. He'd have known whatever leads you had and obviously knew where you lived. Tell me if I'm totally crazy."

Harris looked to Gonzales. Gonzales looked back at Harris. It was clear he hadn't heard any of the phone conversation. Harris couldn't imagine that Gonzales would try to kill him. But nothing seemed right these last few days. And even if Gonzales had been the one to send the package, he wouldn't have known when the bomb would go off. Harris hadn't been at his apartment, he had been staying with his parents, and Gonzales knew he was staying with his parents. A thousand thoughts raced through his mind.

Harris had to think of a way to maintain coded speech, "I don't think so. The file could have been deleted at any time, and besides, they knew that the file was being saved in a different folder." He was hoping that David understood that he was implying that the bomb could have gone off at any time and that Gonzales knew he was at his parents' house.

"Then how did he get there so fast?" David retorted. "If he was there before the medics, it would have been less than a few minutes."

"There was a pop-up notification that showed up from the support team," Harris responded.

"Got it. Well, just a thought. I'm glad to hear I was off. I just want to make sure you are safe. So I imagine we have to cancel bowling now?"

"Sadly. We'll find another time. Thanks again for all the help," Harris replied.

"Of course, I'm always happy to help."

Harris hung up the phone and looked over at Gonzales.

"What's up?" Gonzales asked.

"Oh, nothing. David was having some trouble with his computer and needed help finding an old document. He just didn't want to bore you with all the info," Harris explained, hoping that it sounded believable.

"That's the worst. I hate when that happens. In school, I was writing my final paper when the computer crashed. I never did manage to find the file and had to rewrite the entire thing." It seemed that Gonzales had believed the excuse.

Harris's mind wandered back to the idea of Gonzales being responsible for the bomb. He really didn't see any reason for it. They were working on the case together, after all. Harris pushed it from his mind and mentally marked Gonzales as innocent. At that very moment, Gonzales pulled into a driveway. At the end of the driveway sat a small house. The lawn was dying, with big brown patches everywhere.

"Looks like it needs some water," Gonzales said, gesturing to the lawn.

"You carrying?" Harris asked in response.

Gonzales patted his waist, where Harris could see the outline of his handgun.

"Uh, can you undo my seatbelt? The cast isn't cooperating," Harris said with a laugh.

"Are you sure you can do this, Harris?" Gonzales's voice was willed with concern.

"No, but let's go."

Gonzales sighed, shook his head, then pushed the seatbelt button. At the sound of the click, Harris slid his arm out. They both nodded and went to the door. They knocked and waited, but there was no response. They looked at each other and knocked again. They tried the doorbell and still got no response.

"Was there a phone number attached to that file?" Harris asked, trying to look in the windows.

"Yeah, let me check." He called the number, and they heard a ringtone coming from inside the house. Harris and Gonzales looked at each other again.

Harris pointed at the garage and said, "Any car?"

Gonzales jumped and looked in the window. He nodded his head and said, "Yup."

Harris pounded on the door with his left hand and called out, "This is the police! We've just got a few questions."

Still, they got no response. Harris tried the doorknob and found it unlocked. He raised his eyebrows at Gonzales, who shrugged and drew his gun. "Let's go."

Harris opened the door and was greeted by a putrid smell. He gagged and looked in the foyer. Lying on the floor was another body, and when Harris looked closer at the face, he could tell that it was Carl Gilmore. He felt the side of his neck for a pulse, but there was nothing. They were too late.

"I don't think we are going to get any answers from him today," Harris said, closing his eyes and shaking his head slightly.

Gonzales pulled out his phone and dialed, "This is Deputy Gonzales. I've got to report another murder. Carl Gilmore." Pause. "Uh-huh." Gonzales gave dispatch the address and hung up the phone.

"Come on, Harris, let's wait outside. They'll want the scene left alone."

Harris and Gonzales waited outside, and a few minutes later, the cops arrived. One of the deputies, Wilson, climbed out of his car and came to Harris and Gonzales. "What happened?"

"We were coming to talk to Carl, but we never heard a response. We were pretty sure he was home," Gonzales told

Deputy Wilson, "The door was unlocked, and we let ourselves in. We found him just inside the door, dead."

Deputy Wilson asked, "Did you know that this man was a possible suspect in the case?"

"Uh, ye-" Gonzales started to say.

Harris kicked Gonzales and said, "No. We didn't know."

"We'll take it from here. You have to rest up, Harris. We need you back on the street as soon as possible," Wilson said, pointing at Harris's new cast. "Someone will get an official statement from both of you.

Harris and Gonzales had just finished giving their official statements when they saw an unmarked car drive up. They looked over and saw Halistad climbing out of the vehicle.

The detective looked to the open door, but then he saw Harris and changed course. There was a look of shock and anger on his face, "What are you doing here!" He was already yelling before he was to Harris. "I told you to stay off this case."

"I'm not here as an official. It just so happened that we found a dead body." Harris explained calmly.

Halistad was nearly shaking with anger, "What were you doing here at all!"

"We ha-" Gonzales began, but Harris kicked him in the leg again, and he stopped.

"My mother had known Carl's parents. Apparently, his dad was sick, and my mom wanted me to bring him a casserole."

"So, where's the casserole?" Halistad barked.

"Uh, it's in the car. I put it back in the cooler while we were waiting," Harris lied quickly. "Now, if that's all, the doctor ordered rest, so we'll be on our way." Harris wanted to get them out away from the scene as soon as possible. That way, there would be no more questions.

Harris didn't like lying to Halistad but didn't want to get him and Gonzales in trouble.

While they had been talking to Halistad, the coroner had come and gone from the scene. The cause of death was determined to be strangulation, apparent from the bruises around his neck.

Harris and Gonzales quickly got into the car and sped away before Halistad could ask anything else.

"Why'd you lie to him?" Gonzales asked.

"Halistad told me to stay off the case. If he knew I'd been here hoping to conduct an interview with a potential suspect, I imagine it wouldn't end well.

"What have I gotten into, Harris?" Gonzales asked, more to himself than his partner.

"I'm so sorry. I never should have asked you to drive me here," Harris said apologetically.

"It's not your fault. Someone had to find the body. Why not us?"

"Yeah, I'm still sorry. I know that was hard on you the other day."

Gonzales stopped at a four-way intersection. There were no cars around them.

"Can I level with you, Harris?" When Harris nodded, Gonzales continued, "I was planning on handing in my two weeks' notice today."

Harris was not all that surprised, but still, hearing the words was odd, "And?"

"Well, after today, I decided not to. At least not yet. I can't leave you in the middle of this case, now with your arm as well. Even if a lot of your work is unofficial, I still want to stick it out with you. I'm going to call this whole week in as vacation, and I'll help you with what you need. After that, though, I think I'm out."

"I'll support any choice you make. I hope we can stay connected, though."

"Of course, we will. I appreciate you being there for me over the years." They had been partners for two years now, and had also gone through the academy together.

Harris was about to say something when his phone rang. He looked down and saw that it was the station calling him.

He answered it, put it on speaker, and another deputy started speaking to him.

"Harris, this is Johnson. Do you have a minute?" Johnson was new to the department. He had only been on for a few months. He still had to do a lot of the deskwork and handle phone calls.

"Yeah, what's up, Johnson?" Harris asked.

"We have some information about the explosive. It seems to be a rudimentary pipe bomb. We found a 9-Volt battery, some copper wiring, and metal fragments among the box remnants.

"We also found a trigger that set it all off as soon as pressure was released from it. So when you opened the package, it detonated. You were lucky. The bomb squad found a fraction of a second delay in the fuses, which probably saved your life. We interviewed your neighbor Ms. Guiness. It sounds like yesterday a husky deliveryman continued to knock on your door.

"She opened her door and accepted the package on your behalf. She didn't notice any specific features about the delivery man as he wore oversized sunglasses, and his hat was pulled down over his face. We've talked to all the delivery agencies, and none of them have a record of a delivery to your apartment. The package was too destroyed for any hope of fingerprints, but we'll let you know if anything else comes up."

"Thanks, Johnson, I appreciate it," Harris said. Gonzales was about to say something when Harris waved his hand to silence him. Harris needed a minute.

Once Harris caught his bearing, he called David, hoping the recital was over.

"Wow," David said, "I'm so popular today. What's up?"

"Hey, I'm still with Gonzales, but I need to add another name to your search list."

"Hit me."

"Carl Gilmore. Another hockey player. I'm really starting to see a trend going on here."

"Except you," David pointed out.

"Yeah, but that was probably just to silence me."

"Could be. I just got all the kids to sleep and am hoping on the computer now. I should have that info for you soon."

"Thanks. I'm going to my parents' place now and am going to try and get some rest."

"Okay, get better."

Gonzales drove Harris home and then went with Chuck to get Harris's car. Meanwhile, Petunia helped get Harris set up in his bed with a pillow to prop up his arm. They set up a mini computer station on the nightstand, and Harris had his phone next to it, making sure a call from Gonzales or David would ring through, but he silenced all the others.

All Harris wanted to do now was fall asleep, but the doctor had told him with the concussion, he had to stay awake for at least eight hours. He still had about forty-five minutes to go. He pulled his laptop over and, using a pillow as a table, logged in and looked at the file case of Carl Gilmore.

It seemed lacking, and it didn't mention any connection to the McGrundy case or to the Rosburg case. He looked closer into the Rosburg case and saw that the identity had been officially confirmed. Still pending model number. He added a note to the files about their hockey connections and then signed off. Harris remembered that he still had to file the request form with David for the model numbers to be officially released.

Harris called his mom into the room and asked if she would grab the papers from the printer. Fortunately, Harris was able to use the same CPA by-pass and non-familial forms as before, which saved him a lot of writing. Well, actually, it saved his *mom* a lot of writing. With the broken arm, Harris couldn't do much, so she filled in the forms as he told her to. She scanned the documents for him, and Harris sent the email to David. Harris added a note about the files in the report.

He put his laptop away and was relieved that it was within safe sleeping hours. He was just about to fall asleep when his phone rang.

"Sorry to bother you," David said. "We ran into an issue."

"What's up, David?"

"I got those forms. Thanks. I'll get them sent over. I should have an official report for you by Tuesday. I tried getting your numbers sooner using that passcode I found earlier, and it seems like they noticed the unauthorized login and changed the codes.

"I'm working through the firewalls right now. It's going to be hard, but I'm going to get through this. I'll even pull an all-nighter if I have to. Sorry that it'll take longer to get those numbers."

"That's alright, David. I owe you. I'll talk to you tomorrow." He ended the call.

Despite his desire to clean up from the explosion, he couldn't bring himself to stand any longer and fell asleep still wearing his bloodied and soot-covered clothes.

Halistad was already asleep in his bed when he was woken up by an alert on his phone.

He looked at it and saw there were updates made to the case files. He looked at them and saw that it was on the Gilmore and Rosburg cases. He opened them and saw they were model number requests. He was sure he already knew who filed them, but he checked anyway. Halistad looked back through the case files and saw that Harris had filed more of the reports than any other deputy, or Halistad for that matter.

"Harris," the detective sighed. "I thought I told him to back off. I think he might be better at my job than I am. That might be a problem."

Sunday Morning

Harris heard a sound coming from beside him but couldn't tell what it was. Finally, the sleepiness faded, and he comprehended that it was his phone ringing.

He reached over and realized saw that David had called him again.

"We need to talk," David said.

"Alright, I'm all ears."

"No, we need to talk in person. Can you make it to Nick's game today? It's at 2 o'clock this afternoon. I can send you the address. It's at Kolifax Park, north field."

"I know where that is. I'll be there." Harris didn't know what could be such a concern, but he was intrigued. He looked at the clock and saw that it was already 1200.

Harris sat up and saw that a small television set was in the corner of his room, and a remote was on his nightstand. Harris assumed it was the handiwork of his father. Harris clicked on the TV, and the news came on. "A third murder has occurred. We are waiting on identification. On possibly related news, a bomb has gone off at Deputy Charles Harris's apartment. Harris was one of the deputies working on the previous cases." Harris's academy photo came onto the screen.

"Officials have said that it was a self-detonating package. According to reports, Harris has been hospitalized, and we will keep you informed when more information is available."

He only had a couple hours to get ready, and he wanted to take a shower since he hadn't taken one since the explosion, and he felt grimy.

Harris had his mom help him wrap the cast in plastic wrap and then a plastic bag which she duct-taped in place. Harris took a shower, washing his hair twice. By the time he got out, his mom had already stripped his bed of the blood-stained sheets and remade it with clean ones.

Harris dressed in loose clothes that he could easily pull on with only one arm. Finally, he pulled a baseball cap down over his eyes. If someone was trying to kill him, he, first of all, didn't want to be spotted, and second, didn't want to turn David into a target, given all the assistance he had given. Harris still didn't know who had targeted him, but he didn't want to risk anything.

He went out to the kitchen and found mounds of pancakes ready for him. Petunia told Harris to sit, bringing him maple syrup and butter. She also had a coffee cup for him, still steaming hot.

"Where are you off to, honey? Do you really think you should be going out already?" He could tell she was concerned. But also could tell she wasn't going to stop him.

"David said he needed to talk to me. He made it sound urgent. I'm just meeting him at his kid's baseball game. I'll be safe. I promise, Mom." Petunia nodded her head and topped off his coffee cup.

Harris finished his breakfast and took a coffee to go in a giant insulated cup. He went out to his car, unlocking the door when he realized something. There was no way he'd be able to drive with only one arm. Maybe if his left arm had been injured, he could do it, but there was no way he could operate the gear shift like this.

Harris went back inside and saw that his dad was now at the table eating. Harris looked at his watch and saw that it was already 1345. Only a quarter of an hour until the game.

"Hey, Dad, I don't mean to cut your breakfast short, but I really need a ride. Any chance you could drive me?"

"Sure thing, son," Chuck scarfed down the last few bites of pancakes and poured his coffee into a tumbler. He kissed Petunia on the forehead and grabbed his keys. "Let's go."

"So David invited you to his kid's game?" Chuck asked. "It's been a while since you've talked to him."

"Yeah, I didn't realize that I actually missed him. This is the first time I'll see him in person for several years. He said he needed to talk to me about something but that we needed to talk in person. We were going to go bowling tomorrow, but that won't be happening now," Harris held up his right arm to show his cast. He was relieved, his arm didn't hurt much, and he hadn't even needed to take any of the painkillers the doctor had prescribed.

"I'm glad you reconnected with him," Chuck said.

The father and son team made it to the field just as the first inning started.

"Why don't you head on home, Dad? I'll give you a call when I'm ready to head home, or David can probably give me a ride."

"Alright, stay safe out there. No investigating alone, alright? The next bomb might get you. If you absolutely have to do something, take David with you. Or Gonzales if he's available."

Harris agreed and hurried over to the bleachers. Harris could see David sitting with Millie and two younger kids. He took the bleacher steps two at a time and sat down next to David.

"Hey man, what did you need to talk about? You get some numbers?" Harris muttered.

David leaned over and whispered something to Millie. She leaned forward and looked at Harris, smiling at him with a slight wave. She nodded her head to David.

David gestured for Harris to stand, and they left the bleachers. They walked several yards away from the field and started walking on a small path through the park.

"Sorry, I don't want anyone to overhear us," David said.

"I totally get it. So what's up? Everyone okay?"

"Yeah, for now, at least. It took a while for me to get through the firewalls, but at like 5 o'clock this morning, I finally broke through. I got those model numbers, and I noticed something odd."

"What is it?"

"Both people, Gilmore and Rosburg… they were both Model 353."

Harris was confused, "353? McGrundy was also 353."

"Yeah. And *you*." David said seriously.

Harris took a moment to think, "So, what does that mean?"

"I think someone going after Model 353s. Don't ask me why, but four victims. And they're all 353. We have to trust the trend."

"It just doesn't make sense, though. What type of motive is that?" Harris started thinking of possible reasons but couldn't imagine any.

"A really weak one. But then I got to looking. I broke through a few more barriers and then got to a history of model number requests. I noticed one that seemed a bit backward."

"What was it?"

"A request for every Model 353 in Politopia." He sounded solemn and concerned.

"What! Why would they release information like that?"

"Well, they didn't approve it at first. I found one form first marked from Monday of last week that read denied, but then the very next day, there was the same form that read approved."

"Why would they deny it and then the next day approve it?" Harris didn't know much about the NCD, but that seemed odd to him.

"Well, I did a bit more digging again and noticed something else. Monday evening, there was a login that spiked with a non-approved IP address. I think it's possible someone hacked into the system and forced an approval. I would say that's impossible, but I've done it at least half-a-dozen times in the last week, so it's not all that unreasonable. I guess the National Creation Department needs some better security."

"Okay, so it was approved one way or another. What does that mean?"

"Well, a whole file was released with half-a-dozen Model 353s' names."

"Alright, so who all was on it?"

David pulled out a folded piece of paper and handed it to Harris. Harris read over the document as David summarized it. "Well, McGrundy, Rosburg, and Gilmore were all on it. Two names I don't recognize, and then…"

Harris looked to the bottom of the list and saw 'Charles Harris Jr.'

"You," David said.

"So it wasn't just because of the case. I was always intended to be a victim…" Harris lost himself in his own mind. He had assumed the bomb was because he was close to solving the case, but now… well, now it seemed he would have been a target no matter what.

David said something, but Harris didn't register it. David nudged him with his elbow and said again, "You alright?"

"Yeah, I'm fine. Did the form have the name of the person who requested it?"

"No, it was redacted. I tried getting through it, but it was under some serious security. I can try to get through it. You want me to do that now?"

Harris thought for a moment and then said, "No, for now, we'll watch your kid's game while I let all this sink in."

"Alright." Then David asked, "Have you eaten? I'll grab us all some hotdogs if you'd like."

"That sounds great. Thank you. I'll meet you back with Millie."

"You sure you're okay to walk back?"

"I'll be fine. I need to think for a moment," Harris replied, already lost in his thoughts.

David nodded his head, and Harris walked to the bleachers, finding Millie and the kids cheering. Apparently, Nick had just come to bat and made it to second, bringing two other players home.

"Where's David?" Millie asked.

"He's getting hotdogs," Harris told her.

She nodded and turned back to the game. A few moments later, she looked back to Harris and said, "David hasn't told me much.

I think he's trying to protect me or something. I know he's helping you." Harris started to say something, "No, it's fine. I'm happy you two have started talking again. I just want you to promise you'll keep him safe." She looked pointedly at Harris's cast. "He has a family," she continued, "and we need him." She hugged Davey into her chest and put her hand on Sally's head.

"I'll do everything I can to keep him safe," Harris promised her.

She nodded her head, clearly satisfied. They looked back to the game. The teams had switched, and Nick was now pitching. The runner on second tried to steal a base, but Nick threw the ball to the shortstop, who managed to tag the runner before he could make it back to second base.

The crowd roared. David returned a few moments later with a platter of hot dogs and two bags of sunflower seeds. He sat down and passed around the hotdogs and handed one bag of seeds to Harris. Harris filled David in on what he had missed.

"Remember when we played together," David said, "we used to go through a whole bag of these every game. We claimed they were our good luck charm." David laughed, reminiscing.

"Yeah. I remember. I also remember that when you met Millie, *she* became your good luck charm," Harris laughed back.

"Well, here's to both," David said, putting his arm around Millie and kissing her temple.

An hour later, Harris and David had each eaten three hotdogs, finished a bag of seeds, and then split another. It was the top of the ninth inning, and the teams were tied.

Nick was on the pitcher's mound. There were two outs and two strikes. Nick pitched a fastball.

"Ball!" the Umpire cried.

The ball went back to Nick, and he readied himself. He threw a curve ball, and the batter swung.

"Sti-rike three. You're out!"

The teams switched, and Nick was the first to bat. Two pitches flew, and both times the umpire called, "Ball!"

A third pitch came, and Nick swung the bat, and a satisfying crack could be heard, and the ball flew over the pitcher's head and past the fence.

Nick's team cheered from the dugout as he ran to each base. Harris, David, and his family were all standing, whooping, and hollering.

"Go, Nick!" David shouted.

Nick made it back to home base. That took Nick's team into the lead. The umpire cried, "That's game!" over the din of cheering. Nick's team ran out from the dugout and lifted him on their shoulders, carrying him off the field.

David and Millie each picked up one of their kids and ran over to the field, calling after Nick. Harris hurried after them.

David set Sally down and picked Nick up. "You nailed that, kiddo. I am so proud of you."

"Thanks, Dad," Nick replied sheepishly.

"Great job," Harris said as he fist-bumped Nick with his good arm.

"Thanks," Nick sounded a bit confused, and David picked up the cue.

"Nick, I'd like you to meet your Uncle Charles." Harris felt a knot get caught in his throat. David had just introduced him as Uncle Charles. Harris really questioned why he hadn't kept in closer contact with David. They had been so close.

"Oh, I thought you looked familiar," Nick said, "I've seen you in Mom and Dad's wedding photos."

Harris was about to say something when one of the other kids on the team called Nick over. Nick looked at his parents, and when they nodded, he ran off to his team.

"Millie, you mind if I borrow David for a minute?" Harris asked.

"That's no problem. I'll watch the kids."

David and Harris separated themselves from the group, and Harris said, "I think we need a full team meeting at my parents' house. You, me, my parents, and Gonzales. When can you meet?"

"I can go right now. Do you have a ride? We can take my car. I drove separately from Millie."

"That would be great. You're sure Millie won't mind?"

"Nah. I told her I was helping you with a work thing. I didn't give her any details, but she'll understand."

Harris and David went back to the group just as Nick ran back. "Mom! Dad! Coach said he was going to buy the whole team ice cream since we won. Axel said I can ride with him. Is that okay?"

"That's fine. Just make sure to text us when you get there and when you're leaving," Millie told her son.

"Thanks!" he said and ran back.

David told Millie what the plan was, and, as he had expected, she understood. While he was doing that, Harris texted his parents. *Tell you more later. David and I will be home soon.*

The response was almost immediate. *Okay, I'll start some dinner.*

David helped get Sally in her booster seat and Davey in his car seat. He gave Millie a kiss and waved as she drove away.

Sunday Afternoon

"Let's go," David said to Harris, leading him to his car.

They loaded in the car and drove away. "Any stops?" David asked.

"Maybe. I need to make a call." Harris dialed Gonzales's number.

"Hey, Harris," Gonzales said quickly. "I worked all night, and I got those team records you asked for. It seems there were some pretty significant losses through the years. I managed to get team rosters and printed them out for you. Want me to bring them over?"

"Thanks, Gonzales," Harris said, "I appreciate you doing all that work, but we had some serious breakthroughs. I think hockey was a red herring. We need to talk. I'm with David. You cool if we pick you up?"

"I'm intrigued," Gonzales responded, "I'm just at home alone. Give me five minutes to get dressed, and I'll be ready."

Harris ended the call and gave David the directions to Gonzales's place. He sent another message to his mom: *Gonzales will be joining us too.*

There's more than enough food for everyone, she wrote back.

Six minutes later, Gonzales was in the car wearing a t-shirt from the police academy and cargo shorts. Harris could see that he had his handgun on his waist.

"So, what'd you learn?" Gonzales asked.

"We'll fill everyone in when we get to my parents' place."

Gonzales looked at David from the back seat and said, "So, you're the inside source."

David looked at Harris, who nodded affirmatively. "Yeah," David said, "David Jenson, nice to meet you."

"Same here, Pedro Gonzales," Gonzales nodded his head at David in the rear-view mirror, and David returned it.

They drove in silence the rest of the way, each likely trying to come up with some semblance of a plan. They found Petunia standing over the stove when they got to the Harris house.

"Hello, Mrs. Harris," David said to her.

"Hello, David. It's nice to see you again. And please, call me Petunia." She replied while straining a large pot of pasta. She added a few shakes of garlic powder to a sauce pot and asked, "Is everyone ready to eat?"

"I'm starved," Gonzales said.

Harris and David looked at each other, remembering the hotdogs and sunflower seeds, and smirked. "I could eat," they said at the same time.

Petunia served up five heaping bowls of spaghetti with sauce and pulled out a tray of meatballs from the oven, adding a scoop to each serving. They went to the table, along with a large bowl filled with freshly grated parmesan cheese. They all crowded around the table. Gonzales was sitting in the office chair since there were only four dinner chairs. Petunia had offered to sit in the office chair, but Gonzales insisted.

David said grace, and they all dug in. Harris's mom insisted that they not talk about work until dinner was done. They all happily obliged her.

"Does anyone else watch *Baking World Extreme*," Harris asked. Baking shows were one of Harris's guilty pleasures, and *Baking World Extreme* was one of his favorites. It was the first baking show starring entirely Perfect Specimens that also showed on channels in the "real" world.

"Yes!" David said.

At the same time, Gonzales said, "Religiously, I can't believe Betty was eliminated. Her tiramisu was flawless. And her addition of orange zest was genius."

The conversation dissolved in a discussion of which contestant would win. Now that Betty was gone, it seemed that the favorite was Julian, who had made a lilikoi chiffon pie the last week. They were particularly impressed with Julian, considering he was a Model 642, which primarily led to mechanics.

Petunia insisted that Harris try out for next season, using his Piña Colada cupcakes, but he said he couldn't win with only one recipe.

After they all finished their meals, Petunia cleared the table and ushered everyone to the living room.

Chuck brought out the rest of the Piña Colada cupcakes, and Petunia joined them a minute later. After everyone tried the cupcakes, they seconded Petunia's opinion of them.

"Nick's birthday is next month. Do you think you could make these for his party?" David asked. "He would love them."

"You don't think he'd want something sweeter?" Harris asked.

"Nah, he's actually never been all that much for overly sweet. And these will be great because the parents will also enjoy them. They aren't a sugar overload which means no hyperactive children."

Harris agreed, and when everyone had finished their cupcakes, it was time for business.

Harris began by saying, "To start, we all have to promise to keep this info between the five of us. If any of this leaks out, a lot of us could get in trouble, mainly David. Speaking of which, would you care to fill everyone in, David?"

"Sure," David said. He told everyone what he had been doing, all the way back to looking over his boss's shoulder to get the password, breaking through the firewalls, to discovering that the murderer was targeting 353s. Everyone was silent while he explained.

When Petunia heard about the targeting, she gasped, "Oh, Harris! What if they come for you again?"

"That's what we need to figure out. To be honest, the best-case scenario would be that the murderer thinks Harris died." David said.

"I'll make a call," Gonzales said. He stepped into the living room and dialed, holding his phone to his ear. He spoke for a few moments, and then Harris heard him say, "I love you, too."

He came back to the living room and said, "It's all good. I just talked to Lucy. She works at the news station, and she's going to make sure this gets hushed up. All they'll say is, 'Due to an ongoing investigation, we cannot reveal any specifics.'"

"Thanks, Gonzales," Harris said. He thought for a moment and then said, "Actually could you call her back?"

"Sure," Gonzales replied and dialed the phone. It rang, and Gonzales handed the phone to Harris.

"Hey Lucy, this is Harris," he told her.

"Are you alright?" She asked, concerned, and then continued, "Gonzales told me you need the bombing covered up. I told him we'll make sure there isn't any more info revealed. I don't know if you saw it, but there was one story about it the day of. Most of it was the usual, 'No information as of yet.'"

"I appreciate that," Harris said. "What would happen if you were given an anonymous tip that turned out to be incorrect? You wouldn't get in trouble, would you?"

"Well, I suppose not," Lucy sounded intrigued. "Why?"

"Hang on," Harris told her.

Harris held the phone to his chest and said to David, "I need you to give a tip that you are a friend of Deputy Harris, and from what you have heard, he was hospitalized, and the outlook doesn't look positive. Things turned for the worse from a concussion. He sunk back into unconsciousness and likely won't survive."

Harris handed the phone to him, and David told Lucy what Harris wanted. He ended the call and handed the phone back to Gonzales.

His family looked at Harris confused, and he explained, "Just giving no information won't make the murderer think I died, but this will almost guarantee it. If the murderer becomes overly confident, he might just slip up and make a mistake.

They all nodded in understanding, and David continued, "What are we going to do to try and prevent any more murders?"

"First, I need you to find out everything you can about Model 353, David." Harris said, "I have a laptop in the office. Do you think you can use that?"

"No problem." David disappeared and then hurried back with the laptop under his arm. Sitting on the floor, using the coffee table, he started typing on the keyboard. "This might take a while."

"Okay, what else?" Gonzales asked.

"Well, if we're going off this list as the murder targets," Harris said, pulling the paper out of his pocket, "we should try and get these last two people into protection." He looked down at the report, "Mike Brown and Zeke Benton. Gonzales, do you think you can get an address for them? Try to get them somewhere safe?"

"They can come here," Chuck offered. "We've still got a guest room, and this couch is comfortable enough."

"That sounds great. Thanks, Dad," Harris turned back to his partner. "Gonzales?"

"I'm on it," Gonzales said, pulling out his phone.

"What do you need from us?" Chuck asked.

"I don't know yet. I'm going to scour these files again and see if I can figure something out."

"Just let us know," Petunia said, clearing the cupcake wrappers and heading off to wash the dishes.

Harris looked to David and Gonzales and asked, "Is everyone okay with staying here tonight? I imagine this might be a long night." He looked to his parents, making sure they were okay with the plan. They both nodded in agreement.

"I'll call Lucy and ask if she can watch Buster," Gonzales said.

David grabbed his phone, "I'll let Millie know. Her folks can come over to help her with the kids."

They both made their calls and confirmed they would stay.

They then went back to work.

"Chuck," Petunia said, "Why don't you get the sleeping bags and cots from the garage and set them up?"

Harris, Gonzales, and David worked for a while, trying to find something to help them. After a quarter of an hour, Gonzales said, "Got them. I have phone numbers and addresses for both. Do you want me to go get them? I can call them on the way and explain things."

"That's great, Gonzales. Thanks again," Harris told him. "Make sure to stay in contact should anything go wrong."

"Will do. Do you have a jacket I can borrow? I didn't think I'd be out so late."

"Yeah, take any from the closet," Harris told him.

Gonzales disappeared down the hall and came back wearing one of Harris's high school sweatshirts. He was also wearing one of Harris's baseball caps pulled down far over his head.

Gonzales patted the hat and said, "I didn't think you'd mind me borrowing a hat."

"Of course not," Harris said.

Gonzales was about to head out the door when he said, "Hey! I just realized I don't have a car here."

"Take mine," Harris said and pointed to the entry table, and Gonzales grabbed the keys.

"I should be back within two hours. I'll call you."

Chuck was done setting up the cots and had sleeping bags for each. He started taking pieces of wood and bracing them in the windows. Harris looked at him questioningly. Chuck explained, "We're going to have three possible murder targets in the house. I'm taking every precaution possible."

Harris thanked his dad for his proactive thinking and went back to work. He added Mike and Zeke's names to the file and, when he was prompted with the option, selected for them to be added anonymously. He didn't want Halistad to know he was continuing with the case.

While Harris was waiting for David, he clicked on the news. A female reporter was on the screen, standing in front of Harris's apartment building. Harris could see the window that let into his living room and saw that it was shattered.

"We have been given a tip that the only victim of this explosion was Deputy Charles Harris Jr. We are unsure what caused the explosion or if there are any possible suspects. It is possible the explosion was an accident. Harris is reportedly unconscious in the hospital, and it sounds as though he likely won't survive the explosion. When we have more information, we will make sure to give an update. Now back to you, Tanya." The screen cut to another reporter sitting in the studio. Harris clicked off the news and leaned his head back.

He had nearly dozed off when David called out, "I've got something. I don't know if it's important or not. I'll send it to you now."

Harris opened the link and saw it was a file from the research department in the National Creation Department.

David explained, "It seems that there was a break-in a week ago in the research and development lab, and several vials of serum were broken. The odd thing is they were all 353 serums. No other models were affected. And even more important, *every* available vial of 353 was destroyed. I'm not one to believe in coincidences."

"So there's no way to make any more Model 353? I think this confirms our theory, but it still doesn't answer the why," Harris replied.

"I'm still working on it. These reports are like triple and sometimes quadruple firewalled. I've never seen protection like this before. It'll take some time, but I'll get there."

Harris started to feel the weight of the day as well as the day before. "You all okay if I take a shower and get a few hours of sleep? I just need an hour or two."

"Yeah, man. You go. Take as long as you need," David told him, and Harris's parents agreed.

Petunia wrapped Harris's cast again, and he took a warm shower. Most of his cuts from the shrapnel had scabbed over, and the burns were being appeased by ointment.

He laid down in his bed, on top of the cover, and began to drift to sleep. While halfway between consciousness and slumber, Harris heard a phone ring in the living room. He was about to drag himself out of bed when he heard someone else answer the call.

"This is David. Everything good?" Long pause. "Okay, good job. Harris is resting. I really think he needed it. I'll let him know when he's up." Harris faintly heard muttering from his mother, and David's voice said, "Gonzales got Mike, and they are heading for Zeke."

Harris finally fell asleep knowing one person was in safety and the other would be soon.

Sunday Night

Halistad was sitting at his desk when he got an alert to his email.

"Likely targets, Mike Brown and Zeke Benton…" Halistad read. "Anonymous filing? That sounds a lot like Harris to me. I thought I took him off this case."

Halistad clicked a button on his phone, and his secretary came online, "Connect me to Sheriff Morris," he growled.

"Right away, sir," she replied brightly. She connected him to the Sheriff's personal number.

The phone rang several times, and then Sheriff Morris picked up, "Detective, you have something to report?"

"No, I need to know about a deputy."

The Sheriff was confused and asked, "Which one?"

"Deputy Harris."

"Deputy Harris is on medical leave, Detective. He was a victim of the recent bombing. Hadn't you heard?"

"No, I hadn't," Halistad sounded shocked. He had been surprised to see Harris in a cast at Carl's.

"Is there anything else you need, Detective?"

"I told him to stay off this case, and he had blatantly disregarded a command. He has interviewed witnesses without authorization. I want him entirely removed from the case and blocked from viewing files. The same goes for his partner Gonzales."

"I don't see any justification for that Detect-"

Halistad spoke over him, "Do you want these murders to end or not? Take. Harris. Off. The case." Halistad spoke slowly, emphasizing each word.

"Understood, that will happen immediately."

David shook Harris awake and whispered, "It's the Sheriff. You got several calls from the same number, I answered." David held the phone out to Harris.

He took it and spoke, "Sheriff? Is everything alright? Another murder?" Harris was already worrying about Gonzales. If another target was dead, Gonzales had to be close to it.

"Deputy, I just got a call from Detective Halistad. He told me he requested you stay off the homicide cases and that you directly disobeyed his command."

"Well, I… I wouldn't say disobe-" Harris began.

"He just requested that you be entirely removed from all files and evidence connected to the case."

"But Sheriff, that doesn't seem fair. I haven't hindered the investigation at all."

"Halistad seems to think this is what's best for the case, and I have agreed. He also requested Gonzales be removed. Until your medical leave ends and Gonzales is back from this vacation, database access for both of you will be suspended." Harris tried to interrupt, but Sheriff Morris didn't allow him to. "This is the end of the conversation. Good luck with your recovery." The Sheriff ended the call, and Harris looked at David, defeated.

"What happened?"

"They removed Gonzales and me from the case and the system entirely. I won't be able to do anything with the case."

"Well, not officially, at least." Harris raised his eyebrows at David, who continued, "I've been unofficially looking at government files. You can unofficially solve serial murders using police files."

"I suppose that's true. Next time we hear from Gonzales, we better let him know."

"Sure. You want to get some more rest?"

"Nah, I'm up now. What time is it?" Harris asked.

"About midnight. I was going to call Gonzales in a few minutes to check in. We haven't heard from him in about an hour."

"Let's do it," Harris said, concerned.

They were just dialing the phone when a call came in from Gonzales.

"Does your garage connect to the house?" Gonzales said quickly.

"Yes, why? Is everything okay? Why do you sound so worried?"

"I'll tell you when we get there, open the garage, get as many bandages as you have, old rags, and antiseptic. As soon as I pull in, close the garage. I'll be there in less than a minute."

Harris and David threw open the bedroom door and ran to the garage. Harris yelled to his mom, "Mom! Get the first aid kit, and get to the living room! Dad, get some old towels and cut them up."

Harris pressed the garage button, and the door opened slowly. A few seconds later, a small tan car pulled into the garage faster than it should have, and then it screeched to a halt. It wasn't Harris's car, and he didn't recognize it. Harris reached down and grabbed a tire iron from his dad's tool chest, and David grabbed a shovel. There was a woman driving the car and a man in the passenger seat. Harris and David were about to lift their weapons to swing when they saw Gonzales climb out from the back seat.

Harris dropped the tire iron and hit the button, and the door creaked closed.

Gonzales slammed the car door and yelled, "Faster!"

David dropped the shovel, grabbed the red pull cord, and forced the door closed.

Now that Gonzales was out of the car, they could see that his shirt was off and held against his left shoulder. A dark liquid was dripping from it.

"Gonzales! Are you okay?" Harris turned to the door connecting to the house and called out. "Dad, get in here! Gonzales was shot!"

"I'll be fine. The bullet only grazed me. Get him, though," Gonzales said and pointed to the man in the passenger seat. They could see that he was lying immobile, head folded on his chest. The other man in the back seat and the woman driving now started climbing out of the car. Harris directed them inside, and David rushed to the passenger and, with Chuck's help, pulled him out of the vehicle.

They carried him into the living room and laid him on the floor. David felt for a pulse and pressed his ear against his chest. "Nothing," he said, worried.

"Should we take him to the hospital?" Petunia asked, her voice filled with fear and worry.

"He won't last that long," Chuck said confidently. "Start CPR," he commanded.

David ripped open the man's shirt and began chest compressions.

"Dad, there's an AED at the market across the street. Go get it." Harris said.

Chuck started moving to the door, but Gonzales stopped him.

"No. No going outside. They could come by at any moment. We can't risk it. We have to hope CPR works. Chuck, lock all doors and close the blinds. Petunia, turn off any unnecessary lights" They immediately went to work, and Petunia turned off all the lights except for a small end table light.

David continued with the compressions and then pressed his ear against the man's chest. He shook his head sadly and continued with compressions. Harris took towels and built a dam of them around the man, trying to keep the water soaking out of his clothes from spreading, He could see that David was getting winded, and the compressions weakened.

"I need to swap," David gasped, out of breath. Chuck knelt down beside David. He interlocked his fingers and held them over David's.

"Three… Two… One…" Chuck counted, and without missing a beat, Chuck took over the compressions, and David stood up. They all watched hesitantly. Harris felt helpless. He wanted to help with CPR. He was certified, after all, and even trained others in CPR at camps and local high schools. But there was no way he could help the man one-handed.

Chuck continued with compressions. They went for longer than they should have when suddenly the man took a shuttering breath. Chuck pressed his ear against the man's chest and nodded his head. "He's good. He should make it." Chuck then rolled Zeke onto his side in a recovery position.

Knowing the man was alive, everyone turned their attention to Gonzales. His shirt was entirely soaked with blood now. Petunia had already laid a large beach towel over the couch, and they sat Gonzales down on it. She and Chuck put on medical gloves and removed Gonzales's shirt to view the bullet wound. Harris looked at the wound and saw that it was a significant gash going across the top of his shoulder. Fortunately, the bullet hadn't lodged in his shoulder.

Petunia applied an antiseptic to the wound, and Gonzales flinched. She and Chuck cleaned the wound out and tightly bandaged it. Harris grabbed an old shirt of his, and once his parents were done, he gave it to Gonzales to put on.

David had been monitoring the man on the floor the whole time and reported that he was still doing okay.

"Gonzales, what happened?" Harris asked. Now that things had calmed down somewhat, they could turn their attention to discovering the whole story.

Gonzales sat down on the loveseat and began recounting what had happened. "I got Mike, no issue. When he heard what was happening, he tried sending his wife to his brother's house. She refused, and they waited for me." He gestured to the man and woman that had been in the car and were now sitting at the kitchen table eating bowls of food that Petunia had given them during Zeke's CPR.

"When I got there, they ran out and joined me. I had already talked to Zeke on the phone," he gestured to the man on the floor. "It took a bit of convincing, but finally, he agreed to go with us. However, when we got to his house, I honked, and he didn't come out. I was worried that he was having second thoughts. Mike and I ran to the front door. We pounded on the front door and heard a scuffle inside. I tried opening the door and found it locked. Mike and I went in, and Mike's wife followed after. I heard the water running in the kitchen. We ran there and saw the sink overflowing. Zeke was lying on the floor in a pool of water. The side door was open, and I just barely saw someone dash out. I knew Zeke was a more significant concern, though.

"A lamp was lying next to Zeke, with the cord cut. I unplugged the lamp and pulled Zeke out of the water. I couldn't feel a pulse. I was about to start compressions when a gunshot when off, shattering the kitchen window. Mike and I grabbed Zeke and started carrying him out to the car. We were in the driveway when I heard another shot and then a pain in my shoulder. I looked over and saw a car start driving down the street with a heavily tinted window rolling up. I would have gone after them, but I knew we only had so much time to save Zeke. We hurried to your car, but the tires were slashed. Mike's wife stepped up and noticed Zeke's keys were clipped on his belt. She grabbed them and started Zeke's car. We were just a few blocks away and made it here in less than two minutes. I think we broke about fourteen traffic laws on the way here. Fortunately, we made it in time," he gestured to the slowly breathing Zeke on the floor, slightly shrugging. They all looked at Zeke for a moment and could see his chest still rising and falling.

"Should we call the cops?" Petunia asked, reaching for her phone.

"No!" Harris said, which prompted confused looks from everyone. "We're off the case altogether."

Harris turned to Gonzales and explained, "Halistad demanded it, and Sheriff Morris supported him. We don't have any rights to it. If Halistad finds out we were with a potential target, let alone two, he'll have us fired, possibly jailed."

"If that's what you think is best, honey," Petunia said, "I'll trust you."

"We all will," Gonzales said, and everyone nodded along, putting their faith in Harris.

"What now, then?" Gonzales asked.

"Got a place I can smoke?" Mike interjected, speaking for the first time. His wife, who was sitting at the kitchen table next to him, smacked his arm.

"There will be no smoking in this house. You can go out back. No one should see you there." Petunia said, "Chuck, can you stay with him?" He nodded, and they went out back.

"Mom, can you monitor Zeke and make sure he's progressing well," Harris asked.

Harris then turned to David and said, "We've got some work to do."

David and Harris went to the office and continued their research. After a few minutes, the back door opened, and Mike and Chuck came back in. Chuck came and checked on Harris and David, "Need anything?"

"About a million cups of coffee," Harris told him, and his dad went off on his mission.

"There has to be something…" David said. He sat for a moment, looking at the ceiling. "Hey! I think I might have an idea."

He typed on the computer for a while, went onto the NCD website, and clicked through many tabs. After about four seconds, Harris was utterly lost, but David seemed to know what he was doing.

"I got it. Remember I was telling you earlier that the original specimens Kolifax used lived here?"

Harris responded slowly, "Yeah?"

"Well, the original model for 353 moved to Politopia when it all began," David said.

David showed Harris the document. It was a lot of medical jargon that Harris didn't understand, but he did see at the top that it read 'Specimen for 353: Athlete/Responder.' There was a line on the form that indicated it was for the specimen's name, but it was redacted.

"Any way you can get that name?" Harris asked, pointing at the screen.

"Yeah, I'll have it in just a minute." After a few more minutes of typing and the black bar on the line dissolved, and they read the name 'Herman Philips.'

"I don't know that name, do you?" David asked.

"No, I don't. If I still had access to police files, I could do a search."

"Well, I've already hacked into NCD files. I don't see why I can't get into the police files." David suggested with a shrug and a chuckle.

"If you think you can," Harris said hopefully. He couldn't believe where his life had come to, talking about hacking into police and government files so casually.

David went back to the keyboard and started working through more firewalls. Harris sat in a padded chair in the corner and tried to ignore the sharp itch from inside his cast.

Finally, David broke into the files. "Alright, I'm in. Let's find this guy." Harris hurried over to the computer and watched over David's shoulder. "Okay. Let's see. Philips comma Barney.

Philips comma Deborah. Here it is. Philips comma Herman. Got it."

A file came up, and they began to read it. It spoke extensively about Herman Philips's life outside of Politopia. Apparently, he had been a high-ranking general in the military and had been recruited by Kolifax as a model for athletes, police, and other similar positions. They continued reading and then saw something disheartening. At the bottom of the file, they read one word that ruined all their hopes, 'Deceased.'

"Well, I guess that destroys our theory of him being the killer," David said sadly. "I guess all that was just a waste of time."

"Not necessarily," Harris said. "Dad, come here!"

"The coffee is almost done brewing, son," Chuck called back.

"Forget the coffee, Dad," Harris yelled. "I need to ask you a question."

Harris heard his father hurry down the hall, and his dad asked, "What's wrong? Is everyone okay?" His voice was filled with the type of concern only a parent could display. When he came into the office and saw that everyone was safe, he asked, "Did you figure something out?"

"Maybe," Harris told him. "You were in the military before coming here, right?" Chuck nodded with a raised eyebrow. "Any chance you knew a Herman Philips?"

"Oh, you know I'm so bad with names," Chuck said sadly. "I don't think so. Why? Do you think he's the murderer?"

"I don't think so. It shows here that he's dead." Harris pointed to the computer screen, and Chuck looked over his shoulder. "But we thought there might be something in his past," Harris continued.

"He was the original model for 353, and maybe someone held a grudge against him, and now it has been transferred onto all of the Model 353s." Harris had an idea. "Maybe someone else was in line to be the model, but Herman beat him out?" He didn't think it was all that sound of a motive, but it was the best they had right now.

"Sorry, no. I don't recognize the name," Chuck said sadly. "But I might be able to talk to one of my friends. He might be able to get some info."

"I'd appreciate that," Harris said.

The three of them made their way to the living room and saw that Zeke had been moved to the couch. Mike and Gonzales were nowhere to be seen.

"Mike and his wife went to bed in the guest room, and I sent Gonzales to rest on a cot in your room," Chuck explained. "I'll make that call." Even though it was nearly 0200, with the time change, it was already late morning where Chuck's friend was in the "real" world.

He made the call and was disappointed to discover his friend didn't know the name, but he did get a number where he could get the records of deployment. While Chuck was talking, Harris and David poured themselves cups of coffee, Harris's was black, and David's had a splash of low-fat milk. Chuck dialed the new number and began to explain the situation. Harris and David sat at the table, waiting to hear the results.

While sitting there, Harris heard his mom's phone ring.

"Hello?" Harris heard her say. There was a pause, and then she continued, "Oh, you saw the news? I'm sorry to say I don't have much more information on how Charles is doing." She listened for a moment and then said, "Yes, the hospital is maintaining high security. We all appreciate your condolences." She hung up the phone and dropped it on the end table.

Harris was about to ask about the call when Chuck cried out, "Two weeks! I don't have two weeks." Pause. "Alright, thanks, I guess."

"Sorry, son, I couldn't get anything," Chuck said, turning to Harris.

Hearing her husband's dismay, Petunia came into the kitchen. She was still in the living room and had heard the entire exchange. She took the phone from Chuck. "Let me do it," she said.

Chuck was about to argue, but Harris interrupted, "Trust her, Dad." Harris had a knowing smile on his face, which Petunia returned. Chuck and David looked at each other, confusion filling their eyes.

"Hi," Petunia chirped, "I needed to get some deployment paperwork." Pause. "You see, my husband's birthday is coming up, and I wanted to make a scrapbook for him and wanted to add to it my husband's and his friends' deployment papers. I've managed to track down all of the papers except one."

Pause. "Yes, I see, but his birthday is next week, and I made him the wrong cake last year. How was I to know he hated caramel? Well, what I'm trying to say is this year has to be perfect."

Pause. "Really, thank you. His name was Herman Philips. It would have been about twenty years ago."

Pause. "Oh, you're a doll. Thank you." She told the other person Harris's email and hung up.

She looked at the others. "Never underestimate a frantic mom or a distressed wife," she laughed. "You'll have the email in the morning."

"You're the best, Mom," Harris said. "Also, what was the other call about?"

Sadness flashed across Petunia's face. "It was another condolence call. I've gotten several since the news made it seem you were going to die." She shrugged her shoulders half-heartedly, and Harris could see the pain on her face.

Harris felt guilt wash over him. He hadn't even thought of how the lie would affect his parents. He couldn't imagine what it would be like, to receive a call giving wishes to a dying son, and while Petunia knew Harris was alive and well, it still likely made her think of what it would be like to lose him.

Harris didn't know what to say, but fortunately, David broke the moment for him.

"So, what do we do now?" David asked.

"I think the next step is to get some rest. We've hit a lot of dead ends, and honestly, my mental capacity isn't strong enough right now to figure anything else out. We can take shifts watching Zeke," Harris said.

"No." Chuck said, "*We* will take shifts," and gestured to himself and his wife. "You two need rest."

Harris and David wanted to argue. Harris felt that he shouldn't make his parents do all the work. Petunia had already been cleaning the house and preparing meals for everyone, and Chuck had already prepped the entire house for the group and, to top it off, had saved Zeke's life.

Unfortunately, Harris and David were too tired and had to be honest with themselves. They gave in and went to bed. Gonzales was already asleep on a cot, and David took the second one in the room. Harris fell asleep on his bed without even changing his clothes.

Monday Morning

For the first time in several days, Harris woke up on his own. He yawned and stretched out his good arm. He had fallen asleep with his cast on his face and now had a checker-marked pattern imprinted on his forehead.

Harris sat up and saw David on the laptop. He heard a snore and looked over. Gonzales was still asleep on the cot.

"What are you doing?" Harris asked.

"I remembered something. I think it might help us crack this case. I'll have it in a minute." David said without stopping work. "I can't really talk. I'll let you know as soon as I have it."

Harris shrugged and then heard the sliding glass door open and then close. He looked at David, eyes wide with concern, worried someone was entering the house.

David said, "Mike's smoke break. It's the fourth one this morning."

Harris's shoulders relaxed until he heard a car speed away from the driveway. He and David looked at each other and ran to the backyard. They didn't see anything at first but then noticed the surface of the pool churning. They ran to it and saw that Mike was at the bottom of the pool.

Tied around his ankle was a large cinderblock, which he was desperately trying to untie. David dove into the pool. He began working to untie the knot and then had to shoot himself to the surface to breathe. He dove back down and managed to untie the cinderblock from Mike's leg. David pulled Mike to the surface and pushed him out of the pool.

Mike threw up a mouthful of water and took in a gasping breath. Mike shakily sat up and looked around. David pulled himself out of the pool. He pulled off his shirt and tried to wring it as dry as possible and then put it back on. Harris hurried to Mike and pulled him to his feet. He and David led him inside. Once they were inside, they locked the sliding glass door and barred it with wood.

"Mike. What happened?" Harris asked.

"I don't really know. I was going out for a smoke when someone came up behind me. They pushed me down, and I felt a rope cinch around my ankle. They pushed me into the pool. I kept trying to pull the rope off my leg, but the fibers had swollen. "

"Are you okay?" David followed up.

"Yeah, I am. This helped me finally kick that smoking habit, though, because I'm not risking that again."

"Did you see who it was?" Harris asked.

"No, sorry, I only caught a slight profile. Clearly a man, but that was all I could tell for sure." Mike said sadly.

"Well, why don't you shower up? Feel free to take any clothes from the first door on the left," Harris told Mike.

"Thanks," Mike said, and he left, trailing water behind him all the way to the bathroom.

"There's a shower in my parents' room if you want to shower," Harris told David.

"I'll shower later. I was about to get through the last firewall. I think this could be the final clue." He took one of the towels from the night before that hadn't been used and dried his hair the best he could. When he was done, he wrapped it around his waist and went to Harris's room.

Harris and David started walking down the hall when suddenly the guest bedroom door opened, and Mike's wife popped her head out.

"Where's Mike?" Her voice was filled with fear. "I woke up, and he wasn't there. I assumed he was out smoking, but I thought he would be back by now."

"He's taking a shower," Harris told her. "He's okay, but the killer came after him." Her eye's widened with concern. "David saved him. He's completely fine, though."

"You're sure he's okay?"

"I promise." Harris assured her, "Why don't you head to the kitchen? Feel free to start some coffee. It's in the pantry." She started on her way when Harris stopped her. "By the way, I don't believe I ever caught your name."

"Catrina. Thank you, Deputy Harris," she replied and slipped past them down the hall. She stopped a few paces past them and said, "Oh, and in all the chaos last night, I forgot to mention. That car that left Zeke's place last night. I notice the license plate number. I thought it might help." She reached into her pocket and pulled out a scrap piece of paper, and handed it to Harris. "It was a small blue car."

"That's amazing. Thank you, Catrina," Harris said. Catrina continued to the kitchen.

Harris followed David and continued to the computer that was still in Harris's room. They were surprised that Gonzales was still asleep. "So, what are you looking for?"

"Well, I remembered the request filed for 353s, and I thought finding who submitted that would create a possible clue. Or even answer all of our questions if we are lucky," David answered.

"Good idea," Harris said. They seemed to have an ample number of leads, but none of them were quite able to complete the entire picture. "I'm going to check in on this license plate number."

Harris was about to log into his secure network when he remembered he'd been blocked from them. He figured that it might be worth trying to still log in. He typed in his credentials and pressed enter. An error message appeared on the screen. *Account deactivated.*

"Dang it," Harris hissed. "I guess I'm going to have to do this the old-fashioned way."

Harris began dialing the number and then stopped. "Hey David, do you mind if I ask you a question?"

"Of course. What's up?" David said, continuing to type.

"I just don't know if I'm doing the right thing. Should I still be investigating all of this? Both the Sheriff and Halistad have told me to stay off the case, and now Mike almost died, and there is a strong possibility it was my fault."

David stopped typing and looked at Harris seriously, "How in the world would Mike being drowned be your fault?"

"Well, I brought us all together. We already know the murderer had been following Gonzales, and clearly, he knows that we are all here. It's possible that the only reason Mike drowned was because of me," Harris said, the regret and self-doubt strong in his voice.

"But we saved him. And if you hadn't gone after him and Zeke, well… Zeke would be lying dead in a mortuary right now. Only because of you and the rest of the group is Zeke breathing. You are doing the right thing. Don't let worries cloud your judgment."

Harris nodded and said, "Okay, thanks."

Harris finished dialing the phone number. After going through several departments, and nearly thirty minutes of hold music, he got to the vehicle registration office. "I need to get a plate number run," Harris said when the agent answered the phone.

"Name, please?"

"Well, that's what I'm looking for," Harris said.

"No, sir," the agent said slowly, "*Your* name."

Harris felt like an idiot and said, "Ch- uh. David Jenson."

David looked up at Harris, confused, "Sorry," Harris mouthed to him, waving his hand.

The agent continued, "Plate number Mr. Jenson?"

Harris read the number off and heard the agent typing. "One moment, sir," and he heard hold music play.

"What was that for?" David asked.

"Sorry, I panicked. I didn't want to give my name," Harris explained, cupping his hand over the speaker. "The Sheriff was very clear that I needed to stay off the case. I didn't want it to track back to me and possibly lose my job. Your name was the first one I thought of."

"Got it," David said and went back to typing.

The agent came back on and said, "Looks like the vehicle is registered to a Pedro Gonzales."

Harris was confused and asked, "Could you read that plate number back to me?"

The agent read the plate number back, and it matched the one on the paper. "Thank you," Harris said.

"Is there anything else I can help you with, sir?" Harris could tell from the tone of voice that the agent did not honestly want to help.

"No, that's all. Have a great day," Harris replied and ended the call.

"So, who's the owner?" David asked expectantly.

Harris took a moment and looked over to the still-sleeping Gonzales. "She said it was registered to Gonzales," Harris said slowly.

"What!" David barked. Gonzales rolled over on his cot and then continued snoring. David lowered his voice to a whisper. "So, do you think I was right about the bomb?"

"But why would he shoot himself? And Mike and Catrina both corroborated his story," Harris replied.

Gonzales sat up, wiping the sleep from his eyes. "What are you guys talking about?" Gonzales asked through a yarn.

Harris and David looked at each other, and David shrugged. They both looked back at him. "Uhhh…" Harris said.

"What? Did I drool?" Gonzales said and wiped his chin with the back of his hand.

"No… uh," Harris was trying to find the words to say. "I really want to trust what you say, but several clues have started pointing toward you."

Gonzales shook his head in confusion. "What do you mean point towards me? Wait! You don't mean? Do you two think I'm the murderer? What clues are you even talking about?" Harris felt that he seemed genuinely confused.

"Well…" Harris started but then was at a loss for words. How could he even begin to believe that his partner was the killer? "To start, you were the one to find the second body outside Lucy's, where you just happened to be staying."

"But I hadn't planned that! I had too much to drink and needed to sleep it off. Just because I was at the building doesn't mean I killed him." Harris could see that Gonzales was hurt by the accusation.

David jumped in, "Well, it seemed kind of odd that you made it to Harris's apartment so fast after the explosion."

"I just happened to hear it on the scanner!" Gonzales defended.

"I know. But now, I ran the number on the vehicle Catrina saw driving after someone shot you, and the vehicle was registered to you," Harris said sadly.

"But that's impossible. I saw the vehicle. It was a little blue car. I have a red convertible. And I definitely don't have enough money for two cars. And even if I did, how would I be driving that car while also carrying Zeke? And why in the world could I shoot myself? None of this makes any sense," Gonzales replied frantically.

"I know. I know," Harris responded. "I suppose now we have to add this to the long list of unanswered questions we have."

"So you believe me? I had nothing to do with this," Gonzales asked, his voice filled with worry. Harris and David looked at each other. David slightly nodded his head.

"Yeah. We do," Harris said. "I'm sorry. I never should have doubted you."

"Thanks. Well, being a possible suspect for murder makes you hungry. I need some food," Gonzales said.

"Let's go to the kitchen. I'm sure Mom will be starting breakfast soon." Harris and Gonzales walked to the door. "You coming?" Harris asked David, turning back. Gonzales continued to the kitchen.

"Nah, I want to get this completed," David said, turning back to the computer, "It's a real challenge. I think when the person hacked in to override the denial, they also locked down the name under a top level of security and an encryption. Hey!" David said, looking as though he had an idea. "If the murderer was able to hack into the National Creation Department, I bet they could hack into the vehicle registrations and change the name on the file."

Harris nodded his head, "I suppose that's true. Let's hope it's true."

David whispered, "So you think it could still be Gonzales?"

"I don't think so. To be honest, I don't really know what to think now," Harris said. "But I really don't imagine Gonzales is a murderer." And there wasn't any motive for Gonzales.

When Harris met Gonzales in the kitchen, he found that Catrina was in the living room watching the news. Harris helped himself to a cup of coffee and poured one for Gonzales. Gonzales added a handful of ice, a heavy splash of caramel creamer, and a spoonful of sugar.

Harris took a sip of the coffee and was greeted by a unique flavor. One that he didn't recognize. He cocked his head to the side and looked at Gonzales.

Harris heard from the living room, "I hope you don't mind," it was Catrina, "I added a bit of nutmeg to the grounds. It's always been a habit of mine."

Harris didn't know how he felt that something could have been so easily added to his drink. After all, he had almost been killed mere days ago, and three other near deaths had occurred since then. Zeke, Gonzales, and now Mike had all almost been killed. The Harris family now had welcomed three complete strangers into their home. It wasn't as if any of them really knew anything about them. All they knew was that two of them were Model 353s, and the other one was married to a Model 353.

Catrina could have been the murderer after all. She could have drowned Mike in a jealous rage. The guest bedroom window leads directly to the backyard. And from what Harris had heard, Catrina had been very insistent on coming with her husband and the others.

But Catrina couldn't have shot Gonzales or electrocuted Zeke, Harris thought. And Harris couldn't think of any motives for her to kill any of the others. Harris was sure he had never met her and didn't know why she would want to kill him.

It was still a frightening thought, though. Harris could have been easily poisoned right now simply by adding arsenic or cyanide to the coffee rather than nutmeg. In fact, everyone in the house could have been killed, Gonzales, David, and his parents. All of them. Maybe it hadn't been the most brilliant idea to bring all of the possible victims together under one roof. Didn't it just make them an easier target? The murderer clearly knew they were all at this house. They had already come after Mike. When will they strike again?

Harris just had to hope that the murderer thought that Zeke had died. Hopefully, with the way the media presented the bombing, the murderer had also believed that Harris had been killed in the explosion.

The rational part of Harris's mind eventually kicked in, and he took another drink of the coffee.

"Nutmeg. Huh?" He looked to Gonzales, "I think I finally found something I like added to my coffee," Harris said.

Harris and Gonzales sat at the kitchen table, drinking their coffee. Harris filled Gonzales in on what happened with Mike and realized that was once again proof that Gonzales wasn't the killer.

When Harris and David had heard the car drive away, Gonzales was still asleep on the cot, snoring loudly so he couldn't have drowned Mike.

After Harris had finished telling Gonzales about the morning, Gonzales asked, "So do you think we should all go somewhere else? My place is small, but at least the killer wouldn't know about it. I'm sure we could fit there somewhat comfortably."

Harris thought for a moment and then said, "No, I don't think so. The murderer hopefully thinks I'm dead from the bomb and likely believes Zeke was electrocuted. I'm sure they think Mike is dead now too. I don't know if they recognized you when they took that shot or if they simply aimed wildly. But anyways, they might be watching the house, and we wouldn't want them seeing us all leave."

Gonzales quickly agreed with Harris's opinion. They went back to drinking their coffee in silence.

A few minutes later, Petunia appeared with medical supplies, and she helped to clean and rebandage Gonzales's wound. Harris finally noticed that Zeke wasn't on the couch anymore.

He asked Petunia, and she explained that he had come to consciousness in the night and that she had helped him transition to the master bedroom. Now Chuck was staying up with him.

Harris was upset to hear that his parents had given up their bed, but Petunia had insisted that they were happy to do so. It was the least they could do in a situation like this.

After washing up from redressing Gonzales's wounds, Petunia started breakfast. She toasted two whole loaves of bread and fried a dozen-and-a-half eggs and three packs of bacon. The aroma seemed to be a call to the rest of the house as Mike joined them, having cleaned up and found clothes in Harris's closet to wear. When Catarina saw her husband, she kissed his face, and they went to the living room to sit together. David came out a few moments later with the laptop.

"I figured I could eat and hack government documents at the same time," David said.

Mike turned to the sink to fill a glass with water when Harris noticed the back of the shirt he had borrowed. The back of it read, in a bold athletic font, 'Harris Jr.' He then remembered seeing Gonzales leave the day before, also in one of Harris's old athletic shirts.

"They thought it was me…" he said to himself. Everyone looked at him, and he said, "Gonzales, where's that sweatshirt of mine you wore yesterday?"

"Uhh… it's a bloody mess," he said, "It's definitely ruined. I don't think that you are going to want it back." Gonzales sounded apologetic.

"No, no. It's not that. I want to check something," Harris said quickly.

"It's in the back seat of the car," Gonzales explained.

Harris ran and grabbed the sweatshirt and turned it to read the back. Even through the blood, he could still clearly read the lettering. "Harris Jr.," he muttered.

He ran back to the kitchen and showed them the sweatshirt. "Whoever shot you, Gonzales, thought it was me. They probably followed you in my car, and when you turned around, they saw my name and assumed that it was me. Someone just tried to kill me for a second time."

While Harris was talking, his phone chimed an email alert. He sat down and saw that the email contained Herman Philips's deployment history, along with a few other related files. Harris began downloading the files. He opened the first one, and it was a service history. "Bomb squad," Harris said out loud. "That explains the package bomb." He continued reading. It showed that he had a medical retirement from a deployment-related injury. Nothing particularly noteworthy. He opened the following file. It was a photograph.

It was a photo of Philips. As the image loaded on the screen, Harris heard a voice behind him, "That's him!"

Harris looked back and saw that Zeke was standing behind him, and Chuck was close behind, "What? That's who?" Harris asked.

"That's him. That's the man who attacked me!" Zeke explained frantically. Harris could see the fear in his eyes.

Mike leaned over, holding a piece of bacon, and a look of fear washed over him. "Yeah, I didn't get a super great look, but I think you're right. That looks like who tried to drown me."

"I got it!" David cried out. "Charles, you are never going to guess who filed for this request."

"I think I can," Harris said sadly, "Detective Lewis Halistad?"

"How'd you know that?" David asked, sounding disappointed that he had been beaten to the big reveal. Harris somberly turned his phone towards David. On his phone screen was an image of a man in full military uniform. He was instantly recognizable as a younger Detective Halistad.

Monday Afternoon

"Detective Halistad? But why would he do this?" Gonzales asked, dropping his fork with a clank when he heard the name.

"I don't know, but I'm going to figure it out," Harris said, half to himself.

Harris sat down and began to think. There were just so many pieces that didn't entirely add up, and many still didn't. He felt like he was trying to assemble a puzzle where there was no image, and he didn't even know which side went up.

"I thought Philips was dead?" David asked. "That's what the report said, at least."

Harris didn't hear the question. "But why?" Harris asked aloud.

"What, honey?" Petunia asked.

In response, Harris pulled out his telephone and made a call.

Halistad was driving in his small blue car. He had just finished completing the last thing on his list. He had taken care of everything. Ensuring the serum for more 353s was destroyed, and then finally taking out any of the 353s remaining. It was fortunate that Model 353 had been out of circulation for several years. It had given him a short list to work with, only six targets.

He had seen the dead bodies of Carl, James, and Henry with his own eyes. He saw Harris carrying out Zeke's lifeless body. He even managed to take Harris out with a single bullet. They may have made it to the car, but it would have been too late for Zeke, and Harris would have bled out hours ago. He saw them make it back to Harris's parents' home, but he was sure they had unloaded two corpses from the car. And with the drowning of Mike this morning, he had finished his job. He had destroyed every 353 and had ensured there would never be any more. He had even taken the time to throw the blame onto someone else. He knew how easy it was to run a license plate number, so he had changed his car's registration and made it read that Harris's partner, Gonzales, was the owner. He couldn't help but laugh at his genius.

He continued driving away from the Harris house, heading for the Politopia border, planning on leaving this dystopia and never looking back. He was mere miles from escaping past the border when he heard a phone call come in.

"We need to talk," he heard Harris's voice say.

"You're alive," Harris growled as he swerved the car to the side of the road.

"You bet, and so are Mike and Zeke. Be at my apartment in thirty minutes," Harris demanded.

Halistad thought for a moment. "Or what?" Halistad said through clenched teeth.

"Or you'll live the rest of your life knowing that you failed."

"You'll be alone?" Halistad asked.

"Whatever you say," Harris replied and hung up the phone.

Twenty minutes later, Detective Halistad was walking up to Harris's building. He pressed the intercom for Harris's unit. He didn't hear a response, but the main door clicked open. He hesitated, then jerked open the door and stormed up the stairs. Halistad made his way to the apartment. He knew the way from when he posed as a deliveryman with the package.

Harris's place still had police tape across the door. However, the door itself had not been repaired yet and was leaning against the wall. Halistad ducked under the yellow tape and found himself inside with all the lights off.

"Harris. You told me to be here. So, where are you?" Halistad bellowed into the apartment.

Harris came out of an interior door and switched on the main lights.

"You alone?" Halistad confirmed.

"That's what you wanted, isn't it?" Harris quipped back.

"How are you alive? After the bomb… and the gunshot. You should be dead."

"You screwed up with the bomb. There was a delay in the detonation, just enough time for me to get cover. Though I suppose I should thank you for this," Harris replied sarcastically, holding up his cast. "And that wasn't even me at Zeke's. It was my partner Gonzales. And anyways, you missed again. I suppose you aren't as great as you think you are."

Harris could see the fury in Halistad's eyes.

Halistad was silent for a moment. Harris could see his jaw clenching and unclenching. Finally, Halistad spoke, "So how'd you figure it out? I thought I covered all my tracks." Halistad began pacing as he spoke, sounding as if he was asking himself the questions as much as he was Harris. He began stating all the ways he thought he had cleverly protected himself from being suspected. "I purposely contaminated the knife when I forgot to wipe my prints from it at McGrundy's place. When the witnesses reported someone similar to my description, I changed the evidence to draw attention away from anything that could possibly resemble me. I meticulously studied old crime files, so I could change the style of the murder every time. I chose to start with all of the hockey players to send everyone on the wrong track. I thought of everything. I planned every detail so carefully. I did… I did everything. How could you have possibly known? How did you figure out it was me?"

A smug smile appeared on Harris's face as he replied, "Well, to be honest, I wasn't convinced it was you until about thirty minutes ago. Up until then, everything presented was viewed as a faceless serial killer. Everything changed once I realized all the victims were 353s. The pieces started to practically put themselves into place with that piece of information connecting all the victims.”

Halistad was in disbelief, “How’d you know they were all 353?” It was the first time that Harris had seen Halistad falter in his confidence. “Only McGrundy had been identified. The others were still pending.”

“I have my ways. And after you so kindly told me to stay off the case, I started keeping all of the evidence to myself. Good thing, too. It seems this whole time, I had just been helping you. I had wondered why you wanted me off the case. Were you afraid I’d replace you? Were you just a true loner that didn’t want a partner? Perhaps you wanted all the glory to yourself… but no, all that time, you were just worried I would catch you. Anyways, after we knew 353s were the target, we made the connection of Herman Philips being Kolifax’s model. While we were researching Philips—we found you. We got your service history and your photo. Zeke and Mike immediately recognized you as their assailant. Then when we got the name back on the request for Model 353 names, all the pieces came together.”

“Well, well, well, so you’ve got it all figured out then. Congratulations.” Halistad said with viciousness in his voice. “What’s the point of all this? You said you wanted to talk to me. If you’ve got it all figured out, why didn’t you turn me in? What do you want? And this better be good, because there is absolutely no reason I shouldn't just kill you right here, right now. I can still finish this."

"You're not going to kill me. You wouldn't have stood here wanting to know what I want if you planned on just taking me out now," Harris said boldly, "and let's be honest, shall we? You've already tried to kill me and failed." Harris had really tried to hold back on the snarky comments, but this man had tried to kill him… twice.

"I wouldn't count on me failing again," Halistad barked and took a step towards Harris.

Harris stepped right back at Halistad and began. "Why are you doing all of this? Killing innocent people?" Harris yelled, surprising Halistad with his forcefulness and stopping the detective momentarily in his tracks, "You were considered to be the best of the best, and you helped to create a perfect population. Why did you try to kill them? Why did you try to kill me!"

"Why? Why! Kid, you think you have it all figured out, but you didn't go deep enough into the story. Kolifax is the real monster in this story. That man ruined my life. He stole my life, and then he blackmailed me, so I had to suffer in silence. I had spent years as a homicide detective and then enlisted in the military. I assume you know about my medical retirement if you've already seen my military history. They made it sound as though I had been injured on the job, but that was just a cover-up.

On my last deployment, I had been exposed to a toxin that slowly destroyed my nerve endings and gradually paralyzed me. I went from doctor to doctor with no results. Finally, I was referred to Dr. Kolifax, who assured me he could save me, and that I would be better than ever. I signed the paperwork without even looking at it, and we started treatment.

"Within weeks, I was progressing positively. But then it turned out he had never really cared about curing me. He cared more about creating life and eugenics than he did about me. He told me about his project. I told him I wasn't interested; I didn't want dozens like me running around. That was when he pulled the contracts back out. It stated that treatment would cease if I didn't participate in his research. At this point, he told me if treatments had stopped, my condition would have progressed faster than before, and I would have died within a week. I had no choice but to agree. Later I discovered there were hundreds like me—singers who had career-ending vocal nodules, scientists who had gone blind, and artists and sculptors with crippled hands. We were blackmailed and forced to participate in his new world if we wanted to be cured.

"He told us that we were helping create a new world, but all he actually did was make a better version of us and, in contrast, made us worse off. After forcing me to participate, he then forced me to live in this stupid place. Treatments had to continue, or… well, I would die. He insisted that all his subjects take new names, and he gave me this awful name, Lewis Halistad… but I had no choice but to agree to everything, or he'd stop treating me.

"I handled it fine for the first few years when most of us here were still 'normal,' but then I saw these 'Perfect Specimens' growing up around me, and I never knew which one of them would grow up to become better than me.

"I tried to suppress the anger for as long as possible, but a month ago… I clicked. And you were part of it. Of course, Kolifax changed the appearance of his models each time. But I could still tell you were one of them… nothing but a better version of me. With that drive for success, doing everything needed to succeed, it was obvious. I knew you would replace me within the year, and I just couldn't allow that.

"That's when I got to work. I wished that I could have murdered Kolifax himself. Strangled him to death with my own bare hands. But he was always protected, and I knew I could never get away with killing such an *important* man," Halistad's voice was filled with disgust. "So I decided rather than kill him, I would destroy his creations. I would destroy what he had forced me to become. I started looking for any 353s possible, and it only confirmed my suspicions when I saw you on the list. I knew killing you first, as a cop, would create too much of a fuss. But who would really care about a retired hockey player? But when you started getting in my way, you moved your way up that list. I made that bomb. It's clearly been too many years. There never should have been that delay. It should have taken you out before you could blink. When I saw you at Carl's place, snooping around again, I couldn't believe you were still alive.

"I knew I had to expedite things. I had been at Mike's house, all ready to take care of him, when I saw your car pull up. Mike ran out and got in. I already knew where Zeke was, and I sped there as fast as I could. I thought I'd be gone before you arrived.

When I saw you leaving, I took the shot. But apparently, that was your partner. I assumed it was you with the car and the jacket, but you once again evaded death. I managed to follow who I thought was you and just barely saw the car pull into the garage. Then all I had to do was wait. I assumed you would bleed out, and Zeke should have died from electrocution. I saw Mike go out back several times for a smoke break. He was even foolish enough to go out alone. I knew that was my chance. I acted as fast as I could. But you had to go and get involved in saving those other fools. But now… now… you're alone. And I won't fail this time."

Halistad reached into his jacket and from it withdrew a pistol, and on the end of it was a suppressor. "Now you die for real this time," and he aimed it at Harris's chest.

Harris stood there with a pistol pointed at him, but he wasn't afraid. He saw movement behind Halistad, and from behind the partially closed hallway door came Gonzales, a gun already aimed at Halistad.

"I wouldn't do that if I were you," Gonzales yelled.

Halistad whipped around in shock and, at the same time, fired a bullet. It went into Gonzales's chest, who fell to the ground, unmoving. Halistad turned back to Harris.

"You said you were alone," Halistad barked.

"So I lied. It's not the first time. And besides, I'm pretty sure I don't need to take orders from a murderer," Harris replied with a confident smirk.

In response, Halistad growled and reraised his pistol. Harris stood firm and heard a gunshot.

Halistad felt a blinding pain in his left thigh, and he fell to the ground, firing a shot into the wall. He looked up at Harris and saw a second face appear over him. A face he didn't recognize.

"You have the right to remain silent," Harris said to him and pulled a pair of cuffs from his back pocket, handing them to the other man.

To the man, Harris said, "Cuff him, David, and put a tourniquet on that leg. Good shot."

Harris ran to Gonzales. "You alright, man?"

Gonzales coughed and sat up. "Yeah, I just had the wind knocked out of me. These things are great." He pulled his shirt up and showed Harris his protective vest. Harris had given David, Gonzales, and himself each a vest before they left the house. At the last minute, Harris had also given a pistol to David.

David and Gonzales had been waiting in the hall closet the whole time, filming the entire interaction. They had expected that Halistad would likely pull something. Actually, they had been hoping for it.

After David had heard the shot ring out and saw Gonzales fall, he barreled out of the closet. He fired a shot at Halistad, and it had been just in time. Just as the bullet hit the detective's leg, Halistad had pulled the trigger. Instead of the bullet finding its way to Harris's forehead, it instead wound up in the wall.

Who knew if Harris would have been able to survive a third murder attempt? They say the third time is the charm, but for who? Harris or Halistad.

David had finished cinching a tourniquet on Halistad's leg and stood over him, pistol in hand. Gonzales reported the incident and was told police were already on the way. A neighbor had called in the gunshot.

The first person through the door was Sheriff Morris, who looked at the scene and was about to reprimand Harris and

Gonzales when they tossed the phone to him. "We got your murderer right here. It was Detective Halistad. All the evidence you need and a full confession is on that phone," Harris said.

The time after the confrontation with Halistad had all been somewhat of a blur to Harris. Halistad had quickly been dragged off after a proper medic had cleaned and bandaged his leg.

After Halistad was taken into custody, David, Gonzales, and Harris had to speak with several different deputies, signing multiple statements. David had to file additional paperwork, given that he was the one who fired the gun. Fortunately, he wasn't dealing with any legal issues, given that he was clearly defending Harris's life.

Harris had just finished giving his statement to Deputy Johnson when Sheriff Morris marched over to him. "Harris. What were you doing working a case I had specifically told you to stay away from?" There was a whisper of annoyance in the Sheriff's voice, but mostly, he just sounded curious.

"I'm sorry, Sheriff," Harris said, "I don't really know what made me do it. I suppose I just felt I couldn't let murders go unsolved. It seemed that I was able to put the pieces together faster than others. I suppose that makes sense, though, given that Halistad wouldn't have wanted the murders solved."

"Well, as your Sheriff, I have to say I am furious with you," Sheriff Morris's voice didn't match the words he said. No matter how hard Harris searched, he couldn't find anger in the voice. "I should revoke your badge. And Gonzales's." Harris could feel his stomach drop and felt nauseous. What had he done?

Sheriff Morris looked around the room and then looked back to Harris. "However, it seems that things worked out well. And as someone who was once a young guy in the department, who likely would have done the same thing, I have to congratulate you."

"In fact," Sheriff Morris continued, "it looks as though we are going to be looking for a new homicide detective. Are you interested?"

Harris couldn't believe it. Not only had he managed to not be fired, but he was also offered a significant promotion. It seemed that Halistad had forced the hands of fate, bringing about his fear of being replaced by Harris.

Harris was whole-heartedly about to agree when something deep inside him prevented him from doing so. "I'm sorry, sir. But I can't." Confusion was evident on Morris's face. "In fact, I would like to officially submit my two weeks' notice."

Sheriff Morris was at a loss for words and then said, "I understand. The station will greatly miss you. Please, let me know if there is anything I can do to ever help you, though."

"Thank you, sir," Harris began to step away when he stopped. "Can I cash in that favor now?" He said to Morris with a smirk.

"What do you need?"

"During this case, I was working with an informant. Some of the ways we got information may have been slightly less than legal. I want to make sure that none of the blame goes to him. Should there be any issues, I want to make sure that I am the only one accused. I'll claim that I coerced him into it if it comes to that." Harris couldn't allow David and his family to suffer because of this case. Three families had already lost loved ones. He couldn't let the Jenson's lose a father and husband.

"You mean him?" Sheriff Morris asked, pointing to David, who was still filling out paperwork. Harris looked at Morris, confused. "Don't forget Harris, I've been on the job longer than Halistad, and I'm not a madman." Morris then explained, for Harris's sake. "It's odd that you would have a civilian here with you to confront a likely serial murderer. I assumed he was an integral part of the case."

Harris nodded his head, impressed with his quick deduction. The Sheriff continued, "I'll make sure he doesn't face any kickback from this… and neither will you."

"Thank you, Sheriff," Harris replied gratefully.

He had to wait a few moments for David to finish, and they were finally able to leave the scene.

David drove Harris back to his home... well... his parents' home. But over the last week, he had come to think of their place as his place once again. It was his childhood home, after all. And now, with the bomb damage to his apartment, Harris had decided to stay with them indefinitely.

Gonzales had gone with one of the deputies at the scene to have his gunshot wound properly cared for. The doctor had been surprised to hear that Gonzales hadn't seen a medical professional yet. He said that the bandaging and cleaning of the wound had been done as if by a trained doctor.

After Halistad had been arrested, Harris texted his parents. Now that they knew Mike and Zeke were no longer in danger, everyone could return to their home. Chuck drove Mike and Catrina to their home and took Zeke to the hospital as well. They wanted to ensure he was fully recovered from the electrocution. It seemed that David and Chuck's CPR had been magical, as he had no lasting damage. He just had to limit physical activity for a few days.

After Zeke was released, Chuck drove him back to his house—leaving him his car. Chuck called a tow truck to come to take Harris's car and rode back home in the truck.

When Harris stepped into the house, his parents ran to him and squeezed him tight.

"Oh honey," his mom said, "We were so worried about you."

His father followed up with, "I'm so proud of you."

"Why'd you insist on confronting him alone?" Petunia questioned.

Harris smirked and said, "That's what the sleuth on TV always did." Harris laughed and finished, "And it always worked out for her. Besides, I wasn't alone. I had backup."

"But what if they had been too slow?" Harris's mom's voice was filled with evident dread, showing how worried she was something may have happened.

"But they weren't, Mom," Harris said as he pulled her in for a hug.

"So what now?" Chuck asked.

Harris thought for a moment. He'd like to talk with everyone again and see what everyone wanted to do, but in the end, Harris said, "That's an issue for tomorrow. For now, we sleep." And Harris slept deeper that night than he had in a long time.

Monday Night
Six Weeks Later

It has been six weeks since the arrest of Detective Halistad. The case had gone to trial. The trial had lasted three weeks, yet the jury deliberation had lasted a mere few hours. Combined with the evidence on Harris's phone, the department had recovered the bullet from Zeke's lawn, and testing showed that it had been fired from Halistad's department-issued pistol. Forensics reanalyzed the knife from the McGrundy murder and realized that there was not, in fact, smearing of Halistad's prints. Instead, it was two separate sets. One from the original handling when he murdered McGrundy, and another when Halistad had grabbed it in front of Harris. Finally, the vehicle registration office found the original documents attached to the blue car, and it was registered to Halistad and not Gonzales. To be honest, there hadn't even been a need for a trial at all, but given that Politopia wanted to maintain justice and order, they carried through with it anyways.

Harris was driving his parents' car in the dead of night down the road. He looked over and saw his mother reading a book in the passenger seat. He looked over his shoulder and saw his father sleeping peacefully in the back seat.

He looked in the rearview mirror and saw the blue minivan following him. He could faintly see David driving it, and sitting beside him was Millie. In the back seat were there three kids. Harris knew that behind the van was a small tan car, a red convertible, and a black sedan. The tan car carried Zeke Benton, the convertible held Gonzales, Buster, and Lucy, and finally, Mike Brown and his wife were in the sedan.

Harris, along with his parents and the entire caravan of travelers behind him, had talked about it and decided they needed to leave Politopia. Kolifax wasn't a brilliant scientist or savior of society as he had fought so hard to present himself as. Rather he was a power-hungry man who would do whatever he deemed necessary to fulfill his vision.

Millie had wanted to go to the media, releasing what they knew, but Harris had thought it wouldn't be safe for any of them. How would they ever feel safe if they were to only become the targets of another madman? That was what Kolifax truly was, a madman bent on creating his own world.

Though despite their attempts, it was still revealed the parts each of them had played in the investigation. Part of the population believed that this proved Politopia had never been a utopia and were sympathetic to Harris and everyone's ordeal. The others blamed Harris and the rest for destroying Politopia and villainized their attempts. Fortunately, none of the information that was leaked had to do with Kolifax and his blackmailing of victims. With a little bit of influence, made possible by Lucy, Halistad was presented as a madman by the media, and the population never even knew that he was the original model for 353s. All the world knew was that he was a lunatic who wished to destroy Model 353, and it was explained that no one could understand the thoughts of a criminally insane man.

The one relief Harris had was that Dr. Kolifax never seemed to release a statement on his stance. It appeared Kolifax believed what the media had released and didn't know that the group knew of his questionable medical methods.

Eventually, most of the population forgot about the ordeal, and life returned to normal. It seemed that was how people lived. They would move on to some new scandal if they weren't actively being fed information. Unfortunately, there was still a small fraction of society that couldn't seem to forget the events and maintained what they called a 'righteous anger' towards the group.

Even now, though, Harris and his friends could never leave their houses without attracting attention, either being praised for their actions or hated for them. The entire group, including Harris's parents, had all received death threats from angered citizens.

Sadly, even the children hadn't been spared it. David and Millie had decided to remove their children from school when Nick had been threatened by fellow classmates who followed along with their parents' ideals.

In the end, it was David's suggestion to leave. All of those involved had very quickly agreed to the plan. However, fulfilling the plan wasn't as easy as it sounded. It wasn't precisely simple to leave Politopia. It took extensive paperwork and was a process that could take months at the least. They considered waiting for the paperwork to file correctly, but the tension was growing as extremists became increasingly enraged with Harris, David, and the rest. And with their names being so well known, they knew as soon as they filed the paperwork, their names would once more fill the media, simply adding fuel to the flame of anger.

They decided that they would fulfill their plan in the same way they had solved the murders, under the radar and possibly bending a few rules. Harris, David, and Gonzales researched for days how they could leave, and eventually, they had what appeared to be a usable plan. It was decided that they would travel at night.

The caravan, led by Harris, was driving down a desolate highway when Harris pulled to the side of the road. He knew that just over a mile down the route was a check station at the border. Harris turned off all the car lights, and the others stopped behind him. They all followed his lead, and suddenly the road was in darkness. David stepped out of his car, a flashlight in hand, and came to Harris's door.

Harris rolled down his window, and David said, "About a mile ahead is that utility road I found. Kolifax had it set up so that he could have transports go in and out untracked." After deciding to leave Politopia, David had used his hacking skills again and found a significant chunk of Kolifax's research. It confirmed everything that Halistad had said. One entire file had been research notes written by Kolifax himself. They had considered releasing them but decided that Politopia was no longer their concern. It could deal with its own issue. Along with the research notes, David had found maps of Politopia and, after scouring them for hours, finally found the utility road they were about to use. It was the only non-patrolled route into and out of, Politopia.

"Alright," Harris replied. He looked to his parents, "Mom, Dad, this is going to work. I'll see you soon."

"I know it will," Petunia said sweetly and leaned over to kiss Harris on the cheek. She reached back and tapped Chuck's leg to wake him. They climbed out of the car and loaded into David's minivan.

When they had been devising the plan, the decision had been made that Harris would draw attention to himself so that the others could slip by unnoticed. Despite the road being unmanned, it was awfully close to a major checkpoint, and they didn't want to risk anyone noticing. Harris was confident that the plan would work, but should anything have gone wrong, he didn't want his parents to be caught in the drama. During planning, Harris had made it clear that should anything happen and that Harris wouldn't be able to join them, he wanted David to take care of his parents to make sure they were settled and comfortable in their new life.

While Harris's parents had been buckling into their seats in the third row of the minivan, David had moved down the caravan to ensure that everyone stuck to the plan.

Harris pulled a baseball cap out of his bag and pulled it far down over his forehead. Over the last week, Harris had allowed the stubble of a beard to grow in. After so much time on the news, from both the bombing and the arrest of Halistad, Harris was almost a celebrity. He didn't want the agent to recognize him. He hoped that the shadow of facial hair and a hat would be enough to conceal his identity. Once Harris saw David climb back into his car, he turned on the headlights and confidently drove the last mile of the road.

Harris rolled down his window at the check station and leaned partially out the window. "Hey," he said nonchalantly. "How ya doing?"

"Fine," the agent replied briskly, clearly not interested in small talk. "Do you have papers to leave?"

"Papers?" Harris asked, feigning confusion. "What do you mean? Isn't this the *Burger Emporium*? I just wanted a large order of fries, a burger, and… oh… what the heck, and a medium strawberry milkshake."

The agent looked at Harris, confusion evident on his face, "*Burger Emporium* is about 10 miles back. That way," he pointed,

"Just go back down this road, take a left at the first turn, and then a right, another right, and another left.

"Okay, so that's a right, then a left, another right, and a right?"

"No, left, right, right, left," the agent corrected, clearly annoyed.

"Okay, right, left, right, left. Right? I mean correct, not right." Harris laughed, playing dumb.

Harris could see agitation growing on the agent's face, "No. Left, then right. Right again. And a left."

"Oh… okay. Right, lef-"

The agent interrupted, "You know what, why don't I just write it down for you."

"Thanks," Harris said, and the agent started looking for a piece of paper. Harris heard a ding and looked down at his phone. He read David's text: *All clear, good to go.*

"You know what. I think I got it," Harris said to the agent, "Left, right, right, left, and then it's milkshake time. Thanks for the directions." Harris threw the car into reverse and pulled away.

Harris drove about a mile past the turnoff, sure that the agent would no longer see the lights of his car, and flipped the lights off again. He waited a moment, allowing his eyes to adjust to the darkness. He turned the car around and drove to the utility road.

He pulled off the main highway onto the dirt road and carefully followed it. Eventually, he saw the red lights of four cars ahead, and he pulled past them, putting the car into park. Petunia and Chuck climbed out of David's car and rejoined Harris.

"So, I guess this isn't really a new life for you?" Harris said to his parents. "After all, this is where you were born. Things haven't really changed for you. What will it be like going from a utopia back to the normal world."

"We may be going back to where we were born, and it may no longer be a technical utopia, but at least we have the one thing we want." Petunia reached back and grabbed Chuck's hand. "The one thing we had always wanted." She looked to Harris. "You."

"She's right, son," Chuck said, reaching forward to put his hand on Harris's shoulder. "It may have taken a demented scientist, but the one thing we always knew we needed was a child. And we couldn't have asked for a better son."

Harris had a tear running down his cheek, and he said, "I love you, Mom and Dad."

"We love you too," Petunia said.

With that, Harris started the car's engine and began to drive. The sun was just beginning to rise, and with the sunrise welcoming them, Harris led himself, his family, and his friends into a new life. Into a better life.

Wednesday Afternoon

One Year Later

Life had gone well for everyone in the "normal" world. It may not have been a utopia, but neither had Politopia. Soon after crossing the border, the band of travelers slowly parted ways, each creating their own life and fulfilling their own dreams.

Mike and Catrina had moved to a rural community and started a lucrative farm. Zeke had become a professional quarterback on a successful football team and ended up marrying one of the cheerleaders. The season had just ended, and Zeke had led his team to win the league championship and had been voted Most Valuable Player.

Gonzales and Lucy got married and had twins who they named Charlie and Dave. They asked Harris to be the godfather to Charlie, and David was the godfather to Dave. The two friends happily accepted.

David, Harris, and their families had moved to a big city. Harris had quickly gotten hired on with the local police agency, and after hearing about his success with the murder cases, they offered him a position as a homicide detective. He almost accepted, but in the end, he decided to maintain his position as a street cop, at least for a while. He felt that he could do the most to help society that way.

"You're up, David," Harris said, taking a seat beside his friend.

David quickly took a bite from the plate of nachos and stood up. He picked up his bowling ball, which was multicolored to look like a galaxy. He stepped up to the lane, and sent the ball right down the center, and earned a strike.

David fist-pumped and turned back to Harris. He high-fived his friend as he sat down and picked up his glass, which contained cream soda. "I'm so glad we've started these weekly bowling nights," David said.

"Me too, David. Who would have thought our friendship would have been rebuilt from a series of murders?" Harris laughed.

David chuckled and said, "Yeah, I can't believe it took a homicide for us to talk again. It's crazy to me that all of that was just over a year ago." Harris hadn't realized that it had been so long ago. David continued, "And then you went and got yourself blown up, which kept us from bowling for even longer."

Even once Harris's cast was off, he still couldn't bowl for almost six months while he had to rebuild the muscles in his arm. He had gone to extensive physical therapy to assist in the recovery, but it was still a long process. During that time, he tried to bowl left-handed, but that ended poorly. It had been only somewhat recently that Harris and David had been able to start their weekly bowling days. Now, no matter what their plans were, they made sure to never miss it. From time to time, Gonzales even joined them.

Currently, they were in the tenth frame of their second game. David had beaten Harris in the first game, as he usually did. Harris stepped up, hoping that fate would be different this time.

If he managed to knock down eight pins, he was guaranteed to win. He bowled and only knocked down six pins, ending him with a split. He had only one more chance to win. He bowled, and it went right through the gap of the previously knocked-down pins.

David stepped up to bowl. He exactly tied the game. The two friends both shared a look of disappointment with each other.

"Another game?" David asked.

"Nah, I have to get to work," Harris replied, starting to switch out his shoes.

David looked at his watch and said, "Wow! I didn't realize how long we'd been here. I'd better get to work too. Aren't you getting a new partner today, right?"

"Yeah, some lame guy. Just out of the academy," Harris said. Because of Harris's reputation on the force, not because he was a 'Perfect Specimen' but rather because of his merit, Harris had been promoted to a training officer recently.

The two friends finished changing from their bowling shoes. They packed them and their bowling balls away in their bags and walked out of the bowling alley together.

"How's Millie doing?" Harris asked, feeling in-considerate for not asking sooner.

"She's been getting morning sickness," David said. "It was the same with Nick. That time it only lasted for a few weeks, so let's hope it's the same this time. But other than that, she's doing fine."

"When's the due date?" Harris asked.

"August 12th," David replied. It was less than a month away. "I'd been meaning to tell you, we decided on a name for her," David said, "Charlette. After you."

Harris felt a tear form in his eye, "I don't know what to say. Thanks, man."

"How's *your* wife?" David asked.

A few months after moving to the real world, Harris met a girl named Olivia, and it was love at first sight.

Their wedding had been a few months before, and David had been Harris's best man at the wedding.

"She's doing fantastic," Harris replied. "We haven't told anyone yet, but just last week, we found out that she's pregnant."

David clapped Harris on the back. "Congrats, man, welcome to the world of parenthood. Get ready to never sleep again," he said with a roaring laugh.

Harris laughed back, and they both climbed into their cars, heading off to work.

After leaving the alley, Harris had stopped at the dry cleaners to pick up his uniform. The station he worked at no longer had a complimentary service, but Harris didn't mind. He had found that living in the real world, rather than in a bubble of fake perfection, was more fulfilling to him. Even though there was crime here, that also meant he could help people rather than just write the occasional speeding ticket. Even though a world without crime was ideal, that would never happen, and for now, Harris knew he was doing what he was supposed to.

When Harris arrived at the station, he had changed into his uniform and reported to a meeting. It was to introduce him and his new partner to each other. They got along quite well and quickly made their way to the radio car. Harris was now sipping his coffee, to which he added a dash of nutmeg. He looked to his right at his new partner in the passenger seat. Deputy Jenson was drinking a coffee with low-fat milk and no sugar.

"So, what do you think about your new lame partner, Charles?" David asked sarcastically.

"Eh, a little annoying, but I think he'll grow on me," Harris laughed. "Congrats on actually completing the academy this time," he continued.

"Yeah, I didn't flunk out like last time," replied David. "Stupid pull-ups. I never was good at them. Thanks for helping me with that."

After coming to the ordinary world, David had gotten himself set up with another bureaucratic job, working in some government role. After less than a week in his position, David came to Harris with a request. He wanted to leave the desk job and return to the police academy. For the next several months, Harris had acted as a personal trainer for David, and by the end, David was in near-perfect shape. This time when David went to the academy, not only did he pass, but he was top of the class in almost everything.

Harris and David had only been on their shifts for less than an hour, just enough time for them to get their coffees, when Harris saw a notification appear on his console, and at the same time, a voice came over the radio. "Unit 9-Bravo. Please respond to 1st and Jefferson. We have a One-Three-Nine. Again, that is a One-Three-Nine. Permission to respond Code 3."

David turned to Harris and asked, "Murder?"

"Nah, David," Harris replied, "just a robbery."

Harris pressed 'Acknowledged' on the console and then 'Navigate.' Pressing a button on the console, the siren began to wail, and the lights started alternating red and blue.

David took hold of the radio and spoke into it, "This is Deputies Harris and Jenson. We are en route now."

Now that the only remaining Model 353s, Harris, Zeke, and Mike, were living in the real world, they knew there would never be another like them. It seemed that while Halistad had taken drastic measures, he had succeeded in one thing. Destroying

Model 353. Only, rather than killing them as he had wished, he had instead allowed them to break free from expectation and leave that title behind. After they had crossed the border.

They were no longer Model 353, and with that, Model 353 was destroyed, fulfilling a madman's wish.

Despite their hopes to leave Politopia unnoticed, shortly after, their exodus was the one and only talking point in Politopia. Rather than cause an uproar as they had feared, rather, it gave others the courage to follow after them.

Several other families followed after them, some of the first including Gertrude Heelson and Jimmy's parents. Hundreds of families left, and the idea of Politopia began to crumble. Finally, when superstar Fiona left Politopia, it encouraged the remaining citizens to leave, following after their beloved singer.

The flood of Politopians flooding the real world had almost caused a panic. However, Gonzales, along with Lucy, Petunia, and Chuck, had assisted families in coming from Politopia to the real world and helped them to get set up with jobs and housing. It made the transition much easier for everyone.

Many of the Politopians who came worried they would be outcasts in society, that they would never be able to integrate. They found they were wildly wrong. Easily, they were able to find jobs, and spouses, have children, and overall live a normal life.

No one thought of numbers and specimens anymore. They were just humans.

Dr. Kolifax had mysteriously been found dead one morning. Harris had to wonder if it was of natural causes or if another person with a similar mentality to Halistad had fulfilled their wish.

As the population left Politopia, Halistad had been transferred to a national prison under the highest security classification. Harris had made sure that he was a part of that transition, wanting to ensure that Halistad would never target him or his family and friends again.

Eventually, Politopia faded into oblivion. It appeared that most of those who lived there were unhappy with their lives, despite it being a utopia. Now, Politopia was nothing more than a section in history books, just one more example of a failed utopia.

One of the most well-known works written about Politopia was written by a Model 282, though no one cared about his number. Rather, they cared about the extensive and in-depth writings of Killian Fisher, who had completed extensive research, and conducted interviews with Harris, David, and Gonzales to understand exactly what had happened in the case. Killian had even managed to complete an interview with Halistad, wishing to really pick apart the mind of a killer. Now everyone, from Politopia or not, had read *Model 353: The Killing of a Utopia*. The book made best-seller lists only a few weeks after publication and was added to most universities' required reading lists.

Though, maybe through all of this, there was one thing Politopia had been successful in.

It was an example.

Showing that a utopia wasn't possible. Kolifax had created what he believed to be a perfect society, yet there had still been crime.

And while Halistad may not have been a Perfect Specimen, he was the closest thing to it, at least according to Kolifax. And if a nearly 'perfect' specimen was capable of serial murder, wouldn't a perfect specimen be capable of just the same.

Harris himself shared DNA with Halistad, so does that mean, had the situation presented himself, Harris was just as capable of committing those crimes?

So maybe it doesn't matter how much you try to rid the world of crime. After all, everybody makes mistakes, and there is no such thing as perfection.

Flaws are a part of humanity, a part of society.

But that's where people like Deputy Harris and Deputy Jenson come in. The people who vow to protect and defend. The people who put their lives on the line every day to protect those who can't defend themself.

Acknowledgments

Thank you to all the people who have helped bring this book to reality.

Thank you to my mom for your eternal support and long days helping to edit and truly bring these characters to life. Forever my guide post.

Thank you to Ed for letting me pick your brain and run a million "What-Ifs?" by you. There is no step in your dad.

Thank you to all the great authors who came before, especially Agatha Christie and her amazing Who-Dun-Its?

Angela Lansbury for her fantastic mysteries and the amazing family time she has created for my parents and me.

All my other family and friends who have supported and loved me.

Finally, a special shout-out to Connor Reagan, a true David Jenson.

C.T. Carey

loves all things literature, and
can most days be found with his
nose stuck in a book.

9 781737 572282